REVERSE

The Reverse Novel Series

BOOK ONE

REVERSE

The Reverse Novel Series

BOOK ONE

RIAN N. JENKINS

<u>OTHER PROJECTS</u>

A Queen's Heart
Poetry Anthology Vol. One

A Queen's Anthem
Poetry Anthology Vol. Two

Confessions
Poetry Anthology Vol. Three

A Blessing for the World
Children's (Picture) Book

<u>FUTURE PROJECTS</u>

Eminence
Poetry Anthology Vol. Four

Luke Brown
Young Adult Fiction Novel (Coming of Age Romance Novel)

For
Jessica Mellerson
&
Yvonne Belser,

*Thank you for reminding me of what I was destined to do
from the beginning of time.*

TABLE OF CONTENTS

CHAPTER 1

BROTHERS AREN'T CUTE

Monica James

"Who is that caramel drop at your house?" inquires Sharise, craning her neck to get a better view.

The summertime, southern heat would cause anyone to retreat to where there is air conditioning, which is why I'm relieved Tia and Sharise call me over to them where they are chilling in the shade of their front porch. They always think I'm trippin' because I willingly sweat. It is going down again between the James and Brown clans, which is why we are in my driveway battling it out in another game of twenty-one.

Obviously, they are nosy, and fast, my mom would add. My mom thinks they notice boys a little too much for her liking. Nevertheless, I need Sharise to spell it out. I don't see any caramel drop in sight. Although I need a quick break from the heat, D and I are at another tie-breaker and the next game-point wins.

"Who are you talking about?" I peer up the street in both directions to see if _Mr. Fine_ is walking away.

Maybe I missed him.

The only people I see are the boys, Donovan, his little brother, Nick, and my little brother, TJ, playing basketball in my driveway. Mr. Brown's car is parked in front of my house. They don't even bother parking in the driveway since they know at some point we will play ball. As I keep scanning my surroundings, I take in the rows of single story brick homes with long driveways and manicured lawns.

I know she isn't talking about the younger boys. That would be gross. But who is she referring to? It can't be Donovan because he is my brother from another mother and seeing him as any type of _drop_ is disgusting.

"Are you blind?" Tia scolds. "That boy who's playing basketball in your driveway is fine! How can you not see that?" From her position on the top step, she peers down at me like I lost my mind.

"I guess you *are* talking about D," I hunch my shoulders, confused. I look back over to where the boys are playing to try and see what they see in my homeboy. Right now, his shirt is sweaty because the sun is beaming down on the make-shift court, his sneakers are dirty, and the grimaces he makes as he wrestles the ball away from my little brother don't look *fine* to me. He just looks like Donovan, the boy I've been friends with my whole life.

While gawking at Sharise, who has the same dreamy look in her eyes as Tia, I figure out they are serious. Seriously bugging but serious. They're really acting like this over D. Shaking my head in disbelief, I look back at the boys once more.

"Ewe! Why are y'all trippin' over D?"

"Does the *D* stand for *dang, he's fine*?" Tia gushes while fanning herself with her hands.

"The D is short for Donovan," I retort. Refusing to hide my disgust and shock, I gag. "Is someone secretly recording a Blooper's episode? Is Bob Saget here somewhere from *America's Funniest Videos*?"

"Honey, the only one who is looking crazy or funny is you!" Sharise heckles.

"You have Rico Suave with curly hair playing basketball at your house and you're acting blind like you don't see how gorgeous he is. You definitely need glasses. There's no way I'd have all that," she gestures toward Donovan, "at my house to just play basketball."

"Girl, I would foul him on every play," Tia resounds while high fiving Sharise.

No one would ever guess we are in elementary school from this conversation. We are heading to junior high soon. Girls shouldn't be boy crazy so early, according to my mother. There is nothing wrong with liking boys, but I have to admit Tia and Sharise go a little overboard with their fascination. They can't focus when a cute boy is around. Sometimes all they talk about is boys.

"We've never heard of him. Why isn't he your boyfriend?" Sharise chastises while cutting her eyes at me as I pass by her and Tia on the porch after deciding to take a seat.

Tia laughs so loudly that the boys momentarily stop playing basketball to see what is so funny.

Sharise takes this as an opportunity to wave at the one she declares as one of the finest boys she has ever seen. D simply nods his head and goes back to playing ball. I still don't catch what Sharise sees in D. In my eyes, Donovan Brown will always be D and not Rico Suave.

"It's like the candy man has personally delivered a yummy piece at your doorstep, and you don't know what to do with it. Seriously, you are straight buggin' for not scooping him up," Tia coos before giving Sharise another high five to confirm their foolishness.

"Can we continue this conversation later?" I wipe my face in my shirt, tired of the sweat dripping in my eyes and aggravated by them buggin' over D. "I'm being rude to my company." I get up to make my way back to my house.

"I know you're itching to sweat it out some more," Sharise gags. "I don't know how you do it!"

"And around him," Tia adds while slapping Sharise another high five.

I peer at D again, who still isn't fine, then at our brothers, who *wish* older girls would call them fine.

What am I missing?

D becoming my best friend happened seamlessly. We first met in the womb. Mom said D would kick like crazy in his mom's stomach whenever she was around. Our moms did everything together, including working, shopping, and vacationing. There are plenty of pictures of us at the beach and birthday parties with Donovan right beside me.

Sometimes I wonder if our moms planned on getting pregnant simultaneously to share their first child's experiences. They must have liked sharing their pregnancy the first time because our siblings are also the same age. D and I are two months apart. Our brothers are five months apart.

Donovan fits more with my tomboy side. I'm into sports and anything involving athletics, including basketball, football, kickball, baseball and racing by foot or on bikes down the street. I don't mind getting dirty building forts in the woods or digging trenches for war games. Most of my adventures with D and my brothers take place on the weekends since we attend different elementary schools.

I love playing beauty shop with my dolls, painting my nails, and sneaking to wear my mom's makeup, which is how I bonded with Tia and Sharise. They're all about the girly stuff.

"Since you're making your way back over there, you might as well introduce us to Rico, I mean Donovan, or are you going to be a rude best friend and keep him all to yourself?"

Sharise saunters over to my house without giving me a choice. Tia gallops behind her with a little too much excitement. There is only one Donovan and two of them. I've never known them to share anything , including celebrity crushes, so I'm not sure how this will go.

While trying to wrap my mind around what they see in D, I attempt to run ahead of them to diffuse any drama that may arise from them fighting over him. Before I can introduce them, my mom interrupts the wanna be love connection.

"Kids, lunch is ready." Mom steps out from the garage onto our make-shift basketball court. "Hey, Tia and Sharise. What brings y'all over here?"

"Hey, Mrs. James," Sharise and Tia sing.

"I was about to introduce them to D-Donovan and Nick, Mom," I stammer.

Mom usually calls us from the kitchen window or screen door in the garage. Her voice carries so I wonder why she is out here telling us to come eat. Something is up if she came out here to get us.

"Maybe we can do that another time," my mom declares. "Maybe y'all can hang out tomorrow. Boys, Monica, go ahead in the house and get washed up."

"I guess I'll see you guys later." I hunch my shoulders and slowly make my way into the house, watching everyone leave the court.

"Bye, Monica. Bye, Donovan," Sharise calls out while she slowly walks away backward.

"Bye," Donovan says nonchalantly then runs quickly into the house past me. Is he nervous or just hungry?

"You didn't say bye to me," TJ whines to Sharise.

"TJ, I'm sorry. Hi TJ. Nice shot earlier," Sharise flirts to boost his ego. *She's so fake.*

"Thank you! Thank ya very much!" TJ boasts while strolling into the house backward, cheesing at Sharise.

"If you don't hurry up, get in that house and wash up," my mom snatches my brother, pulling him by his arm into the house.

"Momma, she said she liked my shot. She noticed my shot," TJ continues to boast while patting his chest.

"Yes, she notices a lot. A little too much, if you ask me," she mumbles while still ushering us into the house.

"Cindy, what are you mumbling about?" my aunt, Lisa, inquires. Aunt Lisa is Donovan's mother. She is pouring the drinks at the counter when we enter the kitchen.

I'm washing my hands in the laundry room, right next to the kitchen. While I'm not in her line of sight, I'm close enough to hear my mom. The den opens up to our kitchen and there is a wall to hide anyone watching TV, on the computer or eavesdropping on adult conversations, like I'm doing. As a result, I don't see D, who I assume is on the couch watching TV.

I can hear our brothers playing in the bathroom. Our dads are on the back patio laughing about something and my dad is finishing up on the grill. My mom looks around to make sure none of us are in earshot of their conversation. She looks in the den first and I step into the pantry where she can't see me.

After seeing no one, she utters, "Them fast tail girls—"

"Tia and Sharise? You know that isn't nice, Cindy."

Aunt Lisa is placing the cups on the kitchen table neatly tucked into a bay window, allowing all the sunshine to brighten up the room. It seats four and when we eat dinner there, we have a clear view of the patio and luscious, green backyard surrounded by a chain link fence.

My mom rolls her eyes then gathers the plates that we will pile high with hamburgers, hot dogs, Italian sausage dogs, corn on the cob, and all the other cookout staples already placed in the middle of the table.

"You didn't see the look on their faces when they sashayed over here to talk to *your* son. They're too young to already have that look."

"It's like that sometimes," Aunt Lisa adds then looks back at the dads to see what they are cackling about.

My homegirls have always been boy crazy and my mom detected it immediately. I can't pretend I am not listening anymore and startle my mom in the process when I come out of the pantry. "Mommy, you're right. Tia and Sharise think Donovan is so cute. Weird, huh?"

"What is weird is you hiding in my pantry." My mom clutches her imaginary pearls.

"You don't think my baby is cute?" Aunt Lisa jokes.

Not seeing the joke, I gag on my finger then have a seat at the table.

CHAPTER 2

JUMPING INTO A REVELATION

Monica James

Thankfully, their first attempt at a love connection with Donovan was hijacked by my mom. But sadly from that day forward, it became embarrassingly obvious how determined they were to connect with their Rico Suave. They would ask to come over when they knew Donovan was there. They would never come over when I had other company. Because my mom immediately detected their scheming and didn't play that mess, she made it clear that they aren't allowed at the house if he is there. I'm grateful for it, too. The way they act around him is weird and awkward.

Though I like boys, I still don't understand what they see in D. Maybe it's his light-caramel skin, curly black hair, straight teeth, and average height. His smile and laugh are contagious. I can't stay in a bad mood when I'm around him. Fun is his middle name, and it's easy to get along with him. Donovan is very respectful, too. *Yes ma'am and no ma'am* is how he addresses adults.

He has never been one of those stupid boys who hits or slaps girls then runs away. He comes up with the craziest things to do, like building underground tunnels and forts. He likes anything involving sweat and dirt. Sometimes he chooses those wild, fun, and crazy activities to get rid of Tia and Sharise. Now some might say this is the recipe for the perfect boyfriend, but to me, he's just D.

Around noon a few weeks later, we decided to head to one of our usual spots, the creek. Our moms trust us to take our little brothers with us.

It didn't take Sharise and Tia long to figure out my mom wouldn't allow them to visit when Donovan was there. When Sharise and Tia came bopping over, D and I would have to go into the house or go somewhere else. Eventually, Sharise and Tia began to wait until we came down the street to see their Rico Suave.

I could never figure out how they knew when we were on the go. It was like they had a sixth sense for knowing when D and I were headed out. By the time we were near their house, they would be on the edge of Tia's driveway waiting on their bikes. Her house is two houses over from Sharise's.

"Aren't there bugs and snakes out there?" whines Tia after D and I told the girls we were heading to the creek that borders a row of houses and the woods.

"Don't worry about 'em. I'll protect you," beams TJ.

"It's not that bad," D assures them. "Besides, we go out there all the time. Don't we, Monica?" He is cheesing extra hard while trying to wink his eye at me.

"Yeah, all the time," I hesitate with suspicion, wondering what he is plotting.

Hypnotized by D, Tia and Sharise don't catch my suspicion. They are so mesmerized they forget they are too mature for childish games involving dirt, bugs, or anything else they consider icky. They have images to maintain. It always baffles me because they know D is a typical boy who likes getting dirty and sweaty but they still drool over him.

"Well, I trust you, Don, so please lead the way," smiles Sharise.

I hate it when they call him Don. According to them, Don is short for Don Juan, a nickname he doesn't like. Yes, he has two nicknames: Don Juan to his face and Rico Suave behind his back. It implies he is a lover boy. Because D doesn't think it is a big deal, he isn't going to tell them. I think it's a big deal. It's not his name. It's not who he is. But I won't sweat the issue if he doesn't.

We ride out to our destination with D in the lead. If it is just D and me riding bikes with our brothers, we usually ride behind them. Once, Tia and Sharise were so mesmerized by D they caused a collision with the rugrats. Nick called them the tagalongs and only puts up with Tia and Sharise because his big brother always finds a way to get rid of them.

After that unfortunate incident, we thought it best to let D ride up front with the tagalongs while I trail behind the rugrats.

When we got close to the creek, we park our bikes in the back of the old shed. The only way to get to the other side of the creek is to jump across it.

Oh my goodness, that is how D is going to get rid of Tia and Sharise.

I can't see the divas jumping over a creek, not even for "Don." They have never been out here, so they have no clue they'll have to take the jump of doom. This surprise is going to be too funny.

"So where is this creek, Don?" questions Sharise as she twirls her hair around her finger. As usual, I want to gag. D chuckles to himself. He thinks it is hilarious how they try so hard to get his attention.

"Not too far from here. You're going to like it," D grins.

"I don't know, Don," whimpers Tia, who notices the dust and dirt accumulating on her new sneakers.

"Don wouldn't lead us wrong," coos Sharise.

"If they only knew—" Nick mumbles to me.

"What?" interrupts Tia while looking at Nick suspiciously.

All I can do is chuckle.

"If you only knew how much fun we're gonna have," interjects D. He then gives Nick a pleading look that says *don't blow my cover.*

D never likes hurting people's feelings, so he won't bluntly tell the tagalongs to get lost. Instead, he points us in a direction they normally wouldn't venture, and then they find reasons to leave. He knows they are girly girls, so he always chooses to get dirty.

They are my friends. I don't want to be rude and tell them not to play with us. Thanks to D and his plans, I don't have to break their hearts. What is crazier is D has been doing this for a long time and they still don't get it. A part of me wants to tell them but I refuse to because they'll believe I'm trying to keep D to myself.

"Whatever, D! Last one to the creek is a rotten egg!" Nick shouts as he dashes toward the creek. We all sprint behind him. Tia and Sharise follow closely behind D. As we get closer to the creek, which is really like a deep ditch with a stream, I can hear the sounds of frogs and birds. Tia starts to itch, but Sharise seems to be keeping her cool. I know she wants to scream and run, but she doesn't want to look like a fool in front of D.

"Geronimoooo!" shouts Nick as he jumps across the creek.

Sharise and Tia are both stupefied. I wonder if their eyes are going to fall out of their sockets.

"Awesome jump!" cheers D. "So who's going next?"

Tia looks at Sharise as if to say *I told you so.*

"Umm... where is the bridge?" inquires Sharise.

"Are you blind? There is no bridge! DUH!" shouts Nick. "Do you see a bridge?" His annoyance echoes through the woods.

"C'mon, Nick, be nice. Girls, it's not bad. We jump it all the time," D deflects.

"I'm not afraid of dying," Sharise sasses. She's trying hard to impress D, but I need my girl not to say anything crazy like that.

"What if we fall in there?" snaps Tia, "I'm not getting dirty!"

"You just saw Nick make it over just fine," D says.

"He's a boy!" fumes Tia.

"We've all done it, including MJ, and we're still here," D huffs. D gave me this nickname due to our mutual love for our favorite basketball player, Michael Jordan.

"Monica ain't me, Don!" Tia retorts, rolling her neck so hard I think she might pull a muscle. "No offense, Monica. You can be a tomboy, but Sharise and I don't get down like that."

"Suit yourselves," I sigh while jogging back to the imaginary starting line to gain momentum for the jump. They all watch as I take off and do something I have never done before.

I miss my landing.

"Oh my God! Oh my God! She's going to fall!" shrieks Tia.

Sharise is frozen while Tia keeps looking away and then looking back to see if I have fallen yet. It doesn't help that they see dirt, rocks, and pebbles forming a mini avalanche down to the creek.

I hang on to the root of one of the trees with my feet dangling as I try to find something to push myself up on. My shirt and shorts are filthy from slamming into the side of the creek. Thankfully, nothing got into my hair because my mom would kill me. I haven't switched over to the relaxer yet, and getting my hair washed and pressed is at least a two-day process.

"Grab my hand!" Nick pleads as he reaches out to me.

"MJ, no! You'll pull him over!" D panics. Then he takes a deep breath and calmly advises me, "Just pull yourself up using the root."

I do what he suggests while using the rocks embedded in the dirt for leverage. Finally, after almost losing my footing on the rocks a few times, I pull myself up to the cheers of the boys.

"See!" gloats D with a huge grin. "It isn't so bad after all!"

"Didn't you see she almost fell and—" Tia barks before being cut short.

"But she—" interrupts D.

"Shut up, Don!" Tia screams, determined to be heard. "She almost fell and busted her butt! And, look at her clothes! She's filthy! My mama just bought me this outfit! This is crazy! Y'all are crazy! Sharise, you can do what you want, but I ain't the one!" She stomps off without looking back.

"I can't let her go home by herself, so maybe next time," Sharise adds as she trots off behind Tia. I know she's using the excuse to get out of here. There are plenty of times they'll ditch each other to have fun.

TJ and D both make it across the creek fine while I'm still in shock that I almost fell.

"I know you didn't do that on purpose, but I'm glad you did it to get rid of the tagalongs. I can't stand them!" brags Nick. We all erupt into laughter.

D and I decide to climb up one of our favorite trees while TJ and Nick go to the fort we built a few weeks ago. Another breeze comes through as we rest on one of the branches. I close my eyes and allow the cool air to relieve my temporary discomfort. On hot days like today, we love playing by the creek because there is so much shade and the cool breeze often sweeps across the water.

"What are you thinking about?" D inquires.

When I open my eyes, he is staring at me. He must have noticed me beaming. To confirm my suspicion about him plotting to get rid of the tagalongs, I confess, "I thought it was funny how Tia stormed off with Sharise trailing her."

"That was classic," he chuckles.

"Why do you go through the trouble of getting rid of them? Seriously, why don't you just tell them not to hang out with us?" I swat away a fly.

"Why are you sweating it?"

"I'm not sweating it. Just asking. Can't I ask a question?"

He hunches his shoulders and remarks with a sly grin on his face, "I don't go through any trouble. Every time we decide to do something, they don't want to do it."

He has a point but I don't understand why he can't tell them he doesn't like hanging with them. He reminds me that they are my friends, so I should be the one to deliver the news.

He doesn't know the very last thing I'm trying to do is have Tia and Sharise thinking I want him all to myself. They still suspect I have a secret crush on him, and I have to keep telling them they are wrong. I don't even want to have that conversation with them because it's so dumb.

After D questions me on why they are my friends, I let him know I don't have to explain, then wonder why he is so interested in my circle of friends. I get why he doesn't want to be bothered with them, but what he's not going to do is convince me not to hang out with them because he doesn't see how we connect.

After sitting in silence for an hour or so, the now dirty boys voice their eagerness to eat lunch.

"Yeah, I'm hungry, too." D grabs his stomach like he hasn't eaten for days.

"Hopefully, they are finished grilling by the time we get there." I climb down the tree and jump off one of the limbs. I catch D looking at me again. "Is there dirt on my face or something?" I brush my face.

"N-no," he stammers, breaking his trance and then calling over the boys.

"This isn't the way we came in. Where are we going, D?" TJ wonders.

"There is a bridge over the ditch the owner of the house just built."

"I thought you said there was no bridge!" I gasp.

"From the way we came, the only way across was to jump."

"Which means we could have taken another way!" I swing at him.

"What's the problem?" he dodges.

"You made me almost fall for nothing!" I kick up some dirt in his direction. I don't know whether I'm madder I almost fell or that I forgot there is a bridge. Either way, he is straight trippin'.

He dodged the dirt, too, while looking confused. "But you made it. You never had a problem jumping before." D shrugs off my disgust.

"I don't know what's going on with you today," I throw my hands in the air indignantly.

"Are you blaming me?"

Does he believe he is totally innocent in this mess?

"You did indirectly play into my plan," he chuckles in amusement.

I don't find anything funny.

"D, that isn't right!" I yell, slamming my hands on my hips and rolling my neck.

"What? You mad for real?" he turns from jokester to concerned. I don't think I've ever been this mad at D before.

"Those are *my* friends. I know you're tired of them jocking you, so just be real with them and tell them they can't hang with us. I almost fell for nothing, and that's not cool!" I swing again and connect with his shoulder.

"Why I gotta be the bad person?" He rubs his shoulder. "We are at *your* house, and those are *your* friends. They are not getting the hint. If you are really their friend, *you* would tell them why I do what I do. I don't have to explain myself to them. You do!"

Shocked at him getting mad, I tease, "Did something bite you on your butt or did that tree give you a wedgie?"

Nick and TJ erupt into laughter as we mount our bikes.

D simply gives me a smirk, but he knows I'm right.

"Why are you so uptight?"

Did he forget I almost fell playing into his plan?

"Yes, I do believe what you did was messed up, but you're carrying on like I called you ugly."

"Aye, Nick and TJ, y'all keep it moving." D gets off his bike.

"But Mommy said for y'all to watch us," Nick emphasizes while riding his bike around us.

"Just ride around that hill over there. I'll call you when we're ready. Okay, Nick?" I assure them.

Both are excited to prove they can pop a wheelie. When they take off, D turns to face me.

"I-I don't know how to say this," stammers D.

"Say what?" I nag, hands back on my hips.

D paces back and forth in the worn grass. Finally, he stops to say something, shakes his head, and then starts walking again.

"I know you don't have our hungry brothers popping wheelies in the dirt while my stomach is eating itself as you stomp around in the grass."

"MJ, I really like hanging with you," he finally gets out the words, but I don't get his point.

"Duh! We've been best friends since the womb," I remind him.

"Not like that."

"D, I'm not a mind reader. What are you trying to say?" I protest.

"Just know I like hanging with *you* and only *you* when I'm at your house."

"That's all you had to say."

Why is he acting like he is going to huff and puff then blow someone's house down?

"You don't get it. It's cool," D stomps over to his bike.

I take off on my bike while yelling for the boys to come on. I'm way too hungry to try and understand this boy today. Something must've bitten him.

The following day, Tia, Sharise, and I are chilling on the patio of Tia's house. All three of us are stretched across her parents' chaise lounge chairs sipping on red Kool-Aid. Tia's mom even let us have shades she didn't want any more, so we look fabulous. After gulping my glass of Kool-Aid, I finally tell them what I now realize I should have told them in the beginning. They are my friends. I shouldn't let D play them like that.

"He said what?" scoffs Tia.

"Just don't try to hang with us when he comes over. He isn't feeling y'all like that," I urge them.

"If he ain't feeling Tia or me, he must be feeling you," accuses Sharise.

Screeching laughter bursts from me like a dam before I can get the words out. "Y'all are crazy. You never had a cool homeboy?"

"No," they both assert while sitting up to face me.

"I'm too cute to be playing with a boy," conceitedly brags Tia before whispering, "Kissing him is another story, though."

Embarrassed, I shake my head and declare, "Y'all know D is the homie."

"Are you *sure* you don't like him?" Sharise blurts.

Here they go, thinking I want him for myself.

"No!"

"Well, he likes you. Any boy who says he likes hanging with you and *only you* is someone who really likes you," Sharise leans back on the chair.

"Yes, honey. You better wake up and smell the caramel," Tia sasses before snapping her fingers with Sharise. They are both leaning back with their arms crossed.

I keep replaying the events of yesterday in my head. I see him staring at me the way boys stare at their crushes in those sappy, love movies.

D likes me?

There is no way!

"Sometimes I do have dirt on my face," I conclude while hunching my shoulders.

"Girl, dirt has nothing to do with it. He just wants to be with *you* and only *you*," Tia repeats

Sharise feels the need to reiterate that he *has* seen me at my dirtiest, them at their prettiest and he'd still rather spend time with me than them. They even bring up how my hair isn't always fried and laid to the side like theirs, which is relaxed. My mother isn't in a rush to tame the thickness of my hair. They are trying hard to get me to see something I don't want to believe is true.

"Get with him!" Tia proposes.

I shake my head. I can't fathom it. D thinks I'm cute? And that's supposed to be some kind of win?

If they were talking about Ronnie from New Edition or Hakim from The Boys, I'd be all in. But with D? I just can't get with finding my brother, play or not, cute and there's no way he likes me the way they say he does.

CHAPTER 3

CAN'T HIDE LOVE

Donovan "D" Brown

MJ is my homegirl, my best friend… and so cute. Dang near fine. She isn't like other girls. Whether she is getting down and dirty or cleaned up in a skirt, she looks fly. She's beautiful with her kissable lips, radiant smile, and soul-searching chocolate drop eyes. Everything about her is captivating. From her jump shot on the court to her elegance on the track and even how she pouts when she loses a close game in Tecmo Bowl.

We can jam to the latest R&B like Boys II Men and SWV or hip-hop songs from artists like Pete Rock and CL Smooth. Sometimes we sing along with our parents while they play old school music like Earth, Wind, and Fire. She is my "Vision of Love."

If my boys knew I described her like this, they would clown me. I've been claiming her as my homie from the womb and they don't understand why she isn't my tenderoni. They would call me stupid or say I'm straight trippin' for never steppin' to her. But I couldn't risk it. I knew she didn't look at me *like that*. She thinks of me as a cousin or brother, so I lied to my friends, saying I didn't think she was cute. Normally, it didn't bother me, but it was starting to.

"Yo, if that chick was my homegirl," boasts Louis for the fiftieth time.

"Who?" I pretend again to be clueless while taking another shot at the hoop. Today my parents are having another infamous cookout with family and friends. Everyone brings their lawn chairs to chill in the lush grass. Music blares from inside from my dad's surround sound system that is in the den area. Between dancing, stuffing their faces and laughing, the adults are in their own world. The kids are either playing football, basketball, tag, or eating.

"Who else out here is your homegirl, D?" Louis, who we call Lou, badgers.

"MJ?" I continue to play dumb. Usually, she would be over here with us playing basketball. Grubbing like she ain't ate in days, MJ is sitting next to my cousin, Sonya, probably talking about all kinds of other stuff.

"Remind me, how long have you known her?" Lou scratches his chin for the imaginary facial hair he says is coming in while annoying the heck out of me.

"Why do I have to remind you?" I attempt to shoot the ball again and miss.

"Wow, you seem distracted," Lou mocks. "Maybe it will make more sense if you do." He snatches the rebound then expects me to check back the ball.

"She's been around since the womb."

I don't know why Lou asks me to repeat the phrase. He's made it clear on several occasions that he thinks it's wacker than wack.

"Shut up and play ball, dude," I check the ball into his chest.

"Touchy," he rubs his chest while holding the ball in his right hand. "Why are we playing ball, anyway? We have honey-dips in our midst, homie! Your cousin looking fine, too. Crazy how I peeped Monica before, but today, she's bangin'. One day you will see the light, brotha."

I look in MJ's direction wishing I had the courage to tell her and the world that she is my light. Even with mustard on her cheek, she is extra cute. It never fails, every time I'm out and she's there, someone asks about her. I can't deny her beauty, but I have to shrug it off. Other guys may get offended when they hear dudes talk about their girl and though I want to, I can't. Monica ain't my girl yet. No one can deny she is fine. As long as they are not disrespectful, they can complement her all they want.

"Say what you want about Monica or Sonya. Dude, I'm not like you who hits on every chick passing by."

"Not every chick," Lou snorts.

"What about Yasmine? She looks like—" I howl.

"Shut up, don't remind me," he shudders. "I was trying to kick game to her at night."

"You acting like the stadium is dark, Lou! You was looking at her butt."

"See, she had something going for her."

"You slack dude! Real slack! I ain't going to kick or drop game on Monica, and you ain't, either. You'll get your nose broke again," I say, laughing at the memory of how it happened.

My boy looked shook that whole morning. I knew something was up because he wasn't talking my head off on the bus. I didn't pry, but I would find out.

"Yooooo, I can't go out with Y-Yasmin anymore, dude!" Lou stammers

"Why not?" I wonder.

"She doesn't look so cute in the daylight. A little clingy, too," Lou groans.

We are walking toward our homeroom lines after getting off the bus. Since the weather is still warm, we are allowed to play in the area between the portables and the building. In the middle, there are huge oak trees we sometimes climb, chase each other around or play two-hand touch football. The grassy area is a shaded oasis on the hot days. Ironically, our bus comes right before it is time for us to head inside with our teachers. Most of them are standing at the head of the line taking attendance.

"You stupid and wrong. How you gonna do it?"

"Just wait," Lou has this strange look of determination on his face.

When we finally make it to our homeroom line, I notice how dismissive he is of Yasmin, who is trying to get his attention. It's like he's avoiding her. Her homeroom lines up next to ours. Never knew him to straight diss a girl he stopped or wanted to stop talking to. According to him, he hasn't even broken up with her yet so what is really going on?

"Hey, Lou?" sings Yasmine.

"What up?" he mumbles, barely making eye contact.

"Why didn't you call me back last night?" Yasmine hisses, detecting his rudeness.

"Busy. Why you sweating me?" Lou barks.

"You my boyfriend," Yasmine demands.

I notice he is looking around impatiently. "Yoooo, where are they?" he seethes but not low enough.

"Who? I know you ain't ignoring me, Lou," Yasmine scolds.

"About time!" he explodes at Leanne and Brianne, the infamous drama twins. They come running from the bus loop in a hurry. Their bus must have run late.

"Attention! Attention! Yasmin Lane, we have a special message for you," they sing, "Lou no longer wants to be your boo! Sorry for you!" They prance over to their homeroom line, which is next to Yasmin's.

Everyone in sixth grade hears this bootleg telegram and erupts into laughter. To add to the humiliation, the twins are heckling her from their line. Yasmin is mortified. Her glare looks like she wants to strike him with lightning, her tears would burn through his skin like acid. Before she can choke him out, the teachers come over to see what the fuss is all about. Yasmin races off.

I look down at my homeboy and shake my head in disgust. I'm one of the few who aren't laughing. He doesn't notice at first because he is giving high fives to the other jerks who think what he did was cool.

Finally, he turns around, giving me an incredulous look. "What?"

"You know you dirty. Just ill, man! Did you pay the twins?" The twins are known as the biggest hustlers in school.

I want to punch him. You don't dog a girl out like that. He is not man enough to handle his business. He got girls doing it. Now I see why my mother always side-eyes Lou and why my father emphasizes for me to remember who I'm: a young man of integrity who would tell a young lady if I didn't like her anymore. I'd never string her along or embarrass her.

"I got to buy them cookies during lunch for a week," Lou complains.

"You dirty and stupid," I chastise.

It takes the teachers a while to get everyone under control. Some of the knuckleheads are still chanting Lou's name. As we finally walk to homeroom, we hear, "There he is!"

Yasmine is pointing Lou out to her brother, Damon. He is a third grader but don't misjudge him, he's a tough one.

"You want to embarrass my sister, punk!" barks Damon with a George Jefferson like strut and scowl.

Lou doesn't take him seriously. Dude is super short, but Lou learns that day not to underestimate the short dude. Before Lou could clown him, Damon sucker punches him in the nose. He would have done more damage if Mr. Kendall didn't grab him. I think the female teachers are afraid of the little dude. To be honest, I didn't even think he would punch Lou.

"That's what you get, you little punk! If I see you again, it's on!" Damon rages while being ushered to the principal's office.

Yasmine heckles Lou, "Sorry for you, boo! I guess you're the one who is broke down!" Then she also sucker punches him in the stomach.

Some may call me a punk because I didn't defend my boy, but understand, those Lane kids have to be taking ninja classes or boxing. Their reflexes are brutal and I wasn't getting in the middle of that. Especially since my boy deserved it.

Yasmine is also escorted to the principal's office. While walking Lou to the health room, all the kids, along with Leanne and Brianne, think he is the joke now. I couldn't laugh in front of the crowd. So after school, I clowned him all the way home.

"How you get beat up by a third grader and your ex in less than two minutes, dog?"

"Why you bringing up the past, D? That ain't cool, dude!" He lowers his voice, "Don't tell anyone, but I *still* get nervous whenever I see Yasmin or Damon."

"That was like a month or so ago, dog!" I buckle over in laughter.

"Yo whatever! What is funny to me is how you ain't never tried to mack Monica. Let me mack her!" He lets out a loud heckle that has Monica and Sonya looking at him like he's crazy.

"Why are we back on this? MJ is a good chick! You ain't messin' over her. Bust your head wide open!" I threaten.

"Touchy, touchy, touchy! I guess you *are* diggin' her."

"Mind your business, Lou," I warn him, then throw the ball at his head and miss.

When I started feeling girls, it was the beginning of the fifth grade. They just seemed different. MJ was, and still is, the cutest of them all, though. All of a sudden, I wanted to kiss her. I had dreams about her. I couldn't get her out of my head. Since then, none of those feelings have gone away. Before it didn't bother me when anyone thought Monica was cute, then I started getting irritated with Lou and anyone else for even thinking about talking to her. I knew I had to talk to my dad a few days later while we watched the game together.

"Dad, can I get your advice about something?"

He looks at me strangely. We never talk during the game unless it is about the game. While still staring at me like I have a third ear growing, he turns down the volume. I wish he would keep the volume where it is. I'd feel better with the noise drowning out some of what I was about to say. Even the multiple framed photographs on the wall in our den seem to be listening in. Maybe I'm just nervous or paranoid. I know it's just the two of us because my brother is playing video games in the playroom and my mom is watching TV in their bedroom. Watching sports is our thing, my pops and me.

"It must be serious if you want to talk now." He looks between the TV then me at least twice. Next, he grabs his soda can from the coffee table to take a sip, looking nervous.

"I keep having these dreams," I whisper, looking down the hallway to make sure no one is coming.

He chokes on his soda.

"Dad, you alright?" I hand him a napkin from the stack my mom left on the coffee table.

"You just caught me off guard. What kind of dreams?" He wipes at the soda he got on his shirt and mutes the TV.

"It's always me and a girl."

I watch his eyes widen before he replies, "What are you doing with this girl?"

"Holding hands, kissing."

"That's it?" He seems shocked.

"That's it. That's all you do with a girl, right?"

"I thought you had sex ed this year."

"Not until the spring, Dad. What does that have to do with anything?"

"Never mind. Whew." Dad breathes a sigh and takes another long gulp of his soda. He looks relieved but I'm not sure why.

"Who is the girl?"

"I can't say. She's pretty. It's weird. I never had dreams like this before."

"This must be your first crush." A smile spreads across his face.

"I guess." I look away. *Am I blushing? Do boys even blush?* "Hold up, what is a crush?"

He explains that a crush is someone you are attracted to, someone you think is pretty and nice. I feel like I have to let him know I'm talking about MJ. She's my crush and more than pretty and nice. She is gorgeous and the best friend I've ever had. If he knows it's her, it'll help him see how I really feel and why I'm so confused. Just as I'm gathering the courage to tell him, he probes about when I'm going to reveal my feelings to the girl.

"I don't know how to. That's why I need your advice. Didn't you say Mom was your first... what did you call it? Crush?"

"Yeap, ever since fifth grade, but she didn't take me seriously. I would hit her and run so she could chase me."

"Dad, that's so lame."

"Isn't she your mom? Lame works, son!"

I refuse to hit MJ because the girl can fight. Every now and then she lands a punch and it *hurts*. My dad keeps asking questions and wonders whether or not I'm friends with my crush. I let him know, but I didn't want to tell my dad too much because he isn't a dumb dude. I know I said earlier I wanted to tell Dad who my crush is, but realize I don't know if any of the parents can handle two best friends who play in each other's rooms being boyfriend and girlfriend. I can't reveal anymore information because Dad can put things together and figure out who is the crush.

"How long have you felt this way about her?"

"I don't know. It's like one day she was a girl and then *bam!*"

"I feel you, son. It's crazy how they seem to change. But, in reality, they aren't really changing. We see them differently. It's part of growing up."

"Was Mom your only crush?" I stare at my mom and dad's wedding picture, which is in the middle of the framed photographs.

"Yeah, some people thought I was trippin'. I could only see myself with her. It's not like that for everyone, though. You are young. This girl might not be the only one."

"I don't know, Dad." Switching the subject, I ask, "How do you know the girl is feeling you?"

"The way she looks at you." He looks off at their wedding photo. I guess he's recalling the first time he laid eyes on Mom.

"It's hard to explain because every girl is different. Sometimes you just know. Sometimes you have to be a man about yours, ask her and be okay with her saying she isn't feeling you. I've seen brothers go stupid because they couldn't have the girl they swore was theirs. Too many girls out here to be trippin' off one person. You'd look crazy sweating someone who doesn't even want you. And you look like a stalker. That is not a good look, son."

"Stalker?" I wonder.

"Someone who chases a person who doesn't want to be chased. Always seeks their attention. They have the worst intentions."

"That is like playing tag with someone who isn't playing. Why would anyone do that?"

"Exactly. Glad you got sense. You really feeling this girl?" he asks.

"Yeah, Dad. I said that already."

Throwing his hands up in defense he says, "Okay, don't bite my head off. Maybe you should give her something she likes. You do know what she likes, right?"

I want to let my dad know I'm not new to this. I know what my girl, I mean MJ, likes. When I don't respond, this man has the nerve to offer a ride to Dollar Tree to buy something to impress her. He is straight trippin' if he thinks Dollar Tree is good enough for MJ. I tell him I will let him know, ready to end the conversation. With as much as my mom shops and the way that a brother is very responsible with his allowance, I'm pretty sure I will find something to win her affection and it won't be from the Dollar Tree.

"That's all you want to talk about?"

"Yeah, you can take the TV off mute."

"Cool," he nods his head, turns the game up and refocuses on the action of our favorite team.

I had to take my time to plan how to make my move. I knew I couldn't just roll up on MJ without knowing whether or not she was feeling me. I can't be looking stupid. As much as I don't want to admit it to Lou, our conversation pushed me to finally make that move. If he can't take his eyes off her, I need to stop pretending she doesn't make my heart skip when I see her.

POETIC INTERMISSION

Donovan Brown

I Wish She Could See Me

I see her...
Dimples when she laughs.
I see her...
Stingy with her food,
    cute when rude.
Refusing to smile after a loss.
I see her...
Nikes and Sam and Libby,
Ribbons flowing in the wind.
Shorts, dress or skirt,
cleaned up or in dirt.
I see her...
Braids, cornrows, Shirley Temple curls.
I see her...
Sweat pouring down her face
while stealing bases.
I see her . . .
Walking with her head held high.
Not afraid to challenge any guy.
I see her...
Sweet as Jolly Ranchers,
Stuck to my heart like a Now & Later.
Just wish she would see me.

CHAPTER 4

SURPRISE

Monica James

Two months later, after that infamous conversation with Tia and Sharise, my heart is broken because of the military. Ironically, both of their families are reassigned elsewhere, and I'm starting seventh grade without my dawgs. _Straight up wack._

This is the summer we were supposed to be preparing for Junior High together! Junior high is where we are no longer considered little kids. _Move over elementary school. I'm in junior high, baby._ Junior high means our hair and outfits have to be super fly! Who am I going to coordinate outfits with? Who is going to be my best friends going from class to class? We have multiple classes with different teachers. It would help to have my girls with me. After the semifinals and hopefully the finals in summer track, my mom is sending me to visit my grandmother. Thankfully, my twin cousins, who I haven't seen in a year, are visiting my grandmother, too. That time away will allow me to play and bond with my cousins who are like best friends.

Despite both of our fathers being at work, our moms, who are teachers, have most of the summer off. As a result, they are the ones mostly driving us around to camps and outings. To bring some joy back into my life and chill out for a bit, my mom plans an outing with D's family. Due to our busy schedules, we have not gotten together as much as we used to.

We're meeting up at Chuck-E-Cheese for a day of fun. Going to Chuck-E-Cheese isn't only about the excitement of playing endless games like skeeball, basketball, and whack-a-mole while stuffing your gut with pizza. It is also about who will end up with the most tickets. The competitive nature of me and D's relationship kicks into overdrive here, so we always wage a bet on who can win the most tickets while playing against each other. Sometimes if I'm feeling froggy, I bet all or nothing, kicking the beat down meter and trash-talking onto another level. Today I'm feeling *super* froggy.

By the third game, my blood is boiling. In the midst of the loud music and Chuck-E's band playing another birthday song for some kid who is screaming for joy, I'm baffled. I'm not hearing all the bells, whistles, and sirens going off for me. My determination to win has me losing!

How the heck did that happen?

This was supposed to be a day of fun and I'm straight losing. Everything is going D's way. I mean every game is working perfectly for him, spitting out high scores over and over again. The red lights keep spinning and blinking, signaling the ultimate winner today. D's game has *never* been on point like this.

"Why you so quiet, Monica Jaaaeeeel?" D nudges me, causing me to miss another shot in the free throw contest.

"Dang, Monica," Nick is flabbergasted. Since I don't lose often, I don't lose well so our little brothers are also relishing in this moment.

"Wow! D whooped you!" teases TJ. "What was the bet?"

"All or nothing," D heckles.

"You wish you could wake up from this nightmare on Chuck-E-Cheese Street?" TJ jokes. We all side-eye my brother who just told the corniest joke ever.

"That's okay," Nick pats me on the back. "You can have my tickets."

"Aren't you sweet?" I try to look thankful. "But that's okay. I will be fine."

"This is funny to me!" TJ howls at my pain.

"Someone still loves me. Nick, you are nice, unlike your big headed brother," I retort.

"His big headed *winning* brother," D winks at me. "And nice has nothing to do with a bet. You waged this war. When do we ever take it easy on each other?"

Although he is right, I still pout.

"He doesn't understand how to treat a real woman," brags Nick while popping his invisible collar.

We urge Nick to stop with our blank stares. He immediately folds back down his imaginary collar. I always knew he had a crush on me, butttttttterah I can't do it today. I storm off while D and TJ are rolling on the floor.

"I would let you win!" Nick calls out behind me as I stomp toward our moms. I'm ready to go.

"Where you going, MJ? You quittin'? You punkin' out?" D calls out. "You can't get mad because you got *beat down!*" He runs me down, then jumps in front of me. "I know you are not reneging on our bet. Hand them over," he holds his hands out for my tickets.

"*Shut up, D!*" I swing and miss him but he is able to snatch the tickets away. "You didn't have to snatch them. So rude!"

"Hmm. What should I get with all these tickets? So much to decide." He looks like he's counting money.

Refusing to let him rub defeat in my face, I finally make my way over to our mothers and beg, "Please tell me we are about to go!"

"As soon as the boys redeem their tickets, we will leave. I thought you and Donovan were having a good time?" my mother beams.

"Don't make fun of her, Cynthia," snickers Aunt Lisa.

"Y'all are so wrong." I wag my finger wishing they would stop laughing at my embarrassment. "I'll go wait by the van."

Usually, D and I ride on the back row of seats of my mom's minivan and let the young bucks sit in the middle on our rides home. However, because I'm angry, I sit in the middle by myself. Since the rugrats refuse to separate, they sit in the back row with D, who doesn't bother me. Knowing him, he will wait until he sees I've chilled out.

"Hey, MJ," he whispers after scooting next to me a while later.

"What?" I mumble, not bothering to face him.

"You can't face me?" he chuckles

"Still mad," I huff.

"Even if I have a surprise for you?" he nudges me.

"D, don't play. You just want to—" before I can finish my sentence, I turn around and see the woven bracelet I told him I wanted. Every color imaginable is braided in the bracelet, and it snaps with a neon pink plastic clasp. Amid the stripes and rows of color, bright yellow stars and red hearts circle the bracelet.

"I knew you wanted it, so I got it for you. Here," D whispers as he gently takes my arm, placing the bracelet around my wrist then gently clasps it in place.

I smile and stop hating his guts, or at least I try to. I have received gifts before, but random gifts usually come from family or people who *like me*.

Focus, Monica, you can't let him off that easy.

"Thanks, but I'm still mad at you, *Donovan!*" I turn around swiftly to face the window again, refusing to show my sweet best friend I'm blushing. Then I begin to worry if he can see my reflection in the window.

This is the moment everything came rushing back to me. *What was D trying to tell me when Tia and Sharise stormed off a few weeks ago?* Hold on… Sharise and Tia are right. Boys only do stuff like this when they are crushing on someone. So many thoughts are rushing through my mind.

Does D really have a crush on me?

How long has he felt this way?

Do I have a crush on him?

How will our families react to this?

In the midst of struggling with all these questions, I'm highly aggravated by our brothers doing the pee-pee dance in the back of the van. Despite their pleas to our moms to stop so they could use the restroom, they both refuse because they know our brothers. They kept asking to stop at fast food restaurants, which would end with them getting hungry all of the sudden. Our mothers make it a point to go straight to the house.

As soon as we get to Donovan's house, our brothers rush out of the van since their bladders are about to burst. Mom has to get something from Aunt Lisa. I hear her but I'm not paying attention because my mind is preoccupied with my epiphany: *D has a crush on me.*

"You staying in the van, hon?" my mom repeats.

"Yes, ma'am," I mumble.

"I won't take too long," she assures.

I noticed D taking his time getting out of the van.

"Wait, D," I respond as I grab him by the arm.

"Oh, I'm D now? Someone has chilled out," he teases.

"I chilled out when you gave me the bracelet," I utter, pulling on it, avoiding eye contact.

"Why did you act stuck-up when I gave it to you?" he lowers his tone while sitting on the seat and moving closer to me. *What is he doing?*

"To talk all that junk and still lose? I was… am… humiliated, D. Our moms even laughed at me." We cracked up. "I do appreciate the bracelet." I finally build up the nerve to stare back at him.

What am I feeling right now?

"And?" he nudges me, eagerly waiting for a response.

"And I apologize for acting like a brat about it. Thank you." I notice for the first time D's eyes are beautiful. D is cute... gorgeous really.

Hold up.

What am I saying?

What am I doing?

Why are we moving closer?

Lips are touching.

Lips are still touching.

Is this my first kiss?

Did I just have my first kiss… with D?

I back away abruptly.

"Umm. Wow," he breathes softly.

"Wow!" I slide further away, trying to process what just happened.

Before either of us can react to the kiss, TJ bursts into the van.

"D, what are you still doing here? Your dad is looking for you!" he yells.

"Okay." D looks at me but I turn back to the window again before he leaves.

Tia and Sharise would flip if they knew about this. I'm so confused. What is supposed to happen next? I like boys, but it usually starts with a note, like check yes or no if you like me, not with a gift *and* a kiss. I keep wondering if maybe I like him back, but I'm denying it. It feels gross crushing on my brother but honestly, nothing was disgusting about our kiss. I feel all tingly inside. I didn't want the moment to end. I guess I'll have plenty of time to think it over since I won't see him again for a while.

CHAPTER 5

LOST & FOUND

Monica James

Summer track is keeping me busy so I don't have to think too hard about what is going on between D and I. With the extra practices and keeping up with my brother's schedule, the Browns and James clans haven't seen each other in a while. I'm stressing out a little over the semifinal race. Last year, I placed fourth in the trials. Too close not to make it, which means this year I have to make it.

I'm so ready to smash the 100-meter high hurdles like I did earlier this summer. The semifinal race is the next step before making it to the finals in Florida. Having my coach, fam, and friends behind me is a must! It doesn't help that I don't have my relay team members here. We didn't qualify. Being the pride and joy of my hometown makes my heart thump a little more.

It feels weird not seeing D and his family cheering me on in the stands. We can't attend all of each other's games and competitions because every child is involved in their own activities. We try to make it to the championships or big events for each other but D and his family had to travel to his championship game. My normal cheering squad is divided into smaller fractions because TJ also has a championship game, where Dad is the coach and cheerleader.

Slowly bending down into my starting blocks before the final heat, I remind myself that I can win this race. I've been training for it for months. I want to represent my team, my family, and my city in Florida and I refuse to lose to my nemesis…Daliyah Jennings. The thought of her irritates me, but I can't focus on her. This is my moment.

The starter gun sounds and I take off as fast as I can, feeling good about my pace and knowing victory is a few seconds away. I won the previous heats and this is the last thing I have to do before I qualify for Nationals. Daliyah is hanging close to me, but I'll shake her after this last hurdle.

While hearing my mother, who always screams and yells louder than anyone else, cheer me on, tragedy strikes. I see Daliyah speed up and run almost into my lane before I feel something hit me in my side when I prepare to jump. I tumble hard over the last hurdle. The heat I'm supposed to smash. This race was supposed to take me into Florida as a champion.

Instead, Daliyah crosses the finish line. She has the nerve to look back and flash a smirk to confirm I'm not imagining things. This heifer elbowed me.

We have been beefing since her parents signed her up for the rival track club in third grade after our first meet. Their little girl placed second in the team trials and they weren't having it. She was always the best and they weren't going to let anyone, including me, take her spot. Joining the rival team guaranteed her having the number one spot. Ever since then, we have always exchanged first and second place in any race we competed in together.

Both of us believed we would finish first but never in a million years did I ever think the race would end this way. My pride is beyond hurt.   I always finish my races. I'm so devastated because instead of crossing the finish line, I let some random coach carry me over to the medic station. I badly scraped my arm and knee, so the trainers took off my bracelet to bandage up the wounds. It looks like Daliyah steamed rolled over me. This is a nightmare. I can't remember the last time I tripped over a hurdle.

What is supposed to be the dopest day turned wack. I was literally whacked with an elbow in my side. How did the officials and coaches not see that?

Caught up in my mini depression, I didn't even realize my bracelet was missing until we got back to the hotel. Moping turned into hysteria when I finally realized I lost my bracelet.

"Mommy, we have to go back! Mommy, we have to go back to the stadium!" I beg.

"For what? Baby, I'm tired. Whatever you left will probably be there in the morning," she assures. She doesn't see the tears falling as she is pinning up her hair in the mirror. When she turns around and notices my distress, she asks, "Monica, what is wrong?"

"My bracelet! I left my bracelet!"

"The one D got you a few weeks ago?"

"Yes!" I heave.

"Baby, I'm pretty sure we can buy another one, or he can find another one to give to you."

"I don't want another one, Mommy! I want that one! It is the principle! You know I shower in that thing! We have to go back!"

"First, I need you to calm down." She comes over and rubs me on my back.

Where is the *I Dream of Jeannie* genie? I need her to nod her head, so my bracelet will appear. Mommy isn't feeling my pain, and time is a wasting.

"You don't understand! My life will be over if we don't find that bracelet. I can't go back home without my bracelet. I already lost the race, and now I lost the bracelet. Mommy, we have to go back! If you let me search for it, I can find it! I can't go home without it!"

"Monica, you are tired, and it is beyond hot. We are not calling out a search party for a bracelet. I am pretty sure Donovan will understand that you lost it."

"Mom, I should have been more careful! I should have won today! This was my race! I lost, and I embarrassed myself by falling over a doggone hurdle. I never fall in a race!" I don't feel comfortable telling my mom now that I *know* Daliyah elbowed me. My mom doesn't play about her kids so I just want to focus on the bracelet.

"Baby, it happens. You are eleven! We have plenty of time to redeem this day. You know how many Olympians dealt with shortcomings early, midway, and late in their careers, but they kept going. You can't allow this bracelet to put you in a frenzy." Her attempt to calm me down doesn't stop the tears from falling. Reluctantly, my mom grabs her keys and opens the door. I run out like someone shot off another starter gun.

"Monica, you are acting crazy if you think I'm going to run behind you. Slow down, girlie!"

"What if someone tries to take it?" I shout down the hallway. The elevator moves too slowly, so I run down the stairwell and almost knock over a woman who happens to be in my way as I head out the door. I refuse to apologize because she is Daliyah Jennings's mother. I know that is rude but this matter is too urgent to apologize to the enemy.

"*Monica!*" Mommy scolds then she apologizes to Mrs. Jennings. "Please excuse her, Mrs. Jennings. She's in a hurry, but she knows better." Already out of the door, I don't hear Mrs. Jennings's response.

I jet down to the stadium, which is two blocks away. I will search every trash can, each stadium row, and all the bathrooms until I find my bracelet. When I reach the stadium, I immediately run to the medic station only to find the tent is the only thing standing.

My mom looks for the bracelet at the top of the stadium. I'm in the field looking in the grass, acting like the bracelet is the size of an ant. *Oh my gosh,* it should easily stand out in the grass. The colors are neon. Finally, I slowly jog around the inner field and then the track. As I make my way back to the finish line, my mom is there waiting with a concerned look on her face.

"Sit down, Monica."

"No, I have to check the bathrooms and the stands. Maybe someone dropped it in the trash cans up top," I pray.

"*Sit down!*"

I must have gone insane in the membrane because I had to think about it. You don't think about doing anything when Cynthia tells you what to do. Finally, I plop on the bench and catch my breath.

"What is going on?" She stares at me intently, seeing straight through my hysteria.

"Mommy, I need my bracelet," I say after plopping down next to her.

"I know it is special to you, but you can always get another one," she wipes the sweat off my face.

"It won't be the same," I pout.

"It may not be the same one, but it will be from Donovan. You know he will replace it. Now that I think about it... y'all been acting strange. Usually, when y'all don't see each other, you call one another."

"You know, we have been busy." I look across the field to see if I missed it while avoiding eye contact.

Mom doesn't understand how we have been too busy to at least check in. Her look and tone is telling me she knows something is up but I don't know if I'm willing to admit that the only boy who is allowed in my room has a crush on me and I may have a crush on him.

She mentions being able to see D every day at school, but it isn't making me feel better. If the kiss didn't happen, I wouldn't be so nervous about this upcoming school year.

"Seeing D every day? Having classes with him?" I reply as my calmness quickly turns to hysteria again.

"Monica, you have been beating around the mulberry bush and back again. Out with it, girl. What is really going on with you?" My mother leans back, folding her arms across her chest.

Finally, I look at my mom in the eyes, which are a reflection of mine. Then, breathing in slowly, I whimper, "Promise you won't get mad?"

"I promise," she encourages me to spill my guts without fear of repercussions by holding out her pinky.

We pinky promise and then cross our hearts. "Okay, Mom," I huff and puff while praying I don't blow down the house that D and I have built over the past twelve years. "Remember when we went to Chuck-E-Cheese a few weeks ago?"

"Yes." I find myself looking around the stadium, flashing back to the race.

The crowd was cheering us on and then there were the *OOOOOOOHs* that resounded through the crowd when I fell over the last hurdle. The *OOOOOOOHs* that added more pain to my soul. I'm supposed to be celebrating going to Nationals. And what is adding more pain is I don't know if I will ever find the bracelet or the courage to face D after knowing he has feelings for me.

If anyone can help me figure out this confusion, it is definitely my mom.

"D kissed, I mean... I kissed. We kissed." I quickly crouch down.

"Your first kiss?" She perks up.

"Yes?" Wait? What is happening?

"Okay, so what is the problem?" Did the hysteria jump on her?

"Mom, you don't kiss your cousins," I plead.

"Donovan isn't your cousin. Let's be honest, it was bound to happen sooner or later," she chuckles while leaving me flabbergasted.

"What!" I'm baffled again as I plop on the bench.

She shocks me even more when she shares how Aunt Lisa and her have watched this crush since we were little. Apparently, D shared his food with me when I was the greedy and selfish one. When I had a boo-boo, he would kiss it. Of course, I wasn't having it but he would make sure I was okay. What is even more shocking is she knew all this about D and trusted us to be in the same room together.

"We trusted you, but it was your fathers who changed where y'all could play." She moves my hair out of my face as she continues, "You got me out here sweating out all of my press and curl because of a kiss?"

"Yes! I mean no! I don't know! We haven't talked about it, the kiss."

She drops the bomb that this weekend will end with dinner with the Browns. I need more time to process the decision that she believes I can make.

"You will figure this out, sweetie. I promise you and D will be okay." She holds me a bit longer then wipes more sweat along with tears from my face. "Let's get back to the hotel and get you into the shower. I love you, but you stink!"

"I feel the love, Mom." I slap a wet kiss on her cheek. Suddenly, a thought causes me to panic again. "Please don't tell Daddy!"

Mom is laughing so hard she can't get her words out. When she finally does, she asks "Why?"

"Daddy said any boy who lays *anything* on me will get shot! Daddy can't go to jail! We need the money!"

"Truly, you are suffering from heat exhaustion. Wow! You only want your father for the money. Where is the love, Monica?"

"Please don't tell Daddy, Mom!"

"I won't tell him. Honestly, your father won't shoot D. He may shoot those other jokers who try to hit on our baby but not D. If we are being honest, your daddy ain't going to shoot anyone. All fathers protect their daughters by saying that. My daddy did. Besides, every parent wants their daughter to meet a young man like Donovan and not any of those ratnecks."

"Mommy," I choke on my laughter. "Oh my gosh! It's ruffnecks."

"Whatever. Let's go." She pulls me up.

"Can I at least check the ladies' room?"

"Monica, you're testing me. Running in this heat behind a bracelet has me getting my workout in on an off day! It's too hot for all of this. And, I need to set a hair appointment for Tuesday."

"You going to schedule me one, too, right?"

"I should make you rock the puff! Did you know you almost knocked over Daliyah Jennings's mother in the lobby?" she asks as we head toward the stadium stairs that leads us back to our hotel.

"Yep!"

"I'm ashamed!"

"Momma, I know you don't like the mother of the girl who just elbowed me on the track."

"She hit you?" She stops mid step and I regret letting that slip.

"Yes, and I don't know how the refs didn't see it. I can't wait until track season in the spring. I'm going to beat her down!" My mom gives me the side-eye. "On the track, Momma. On the track."

While we are trekking it back to the hotel, my mom lets it be known she will have my coach launch an investigation. She will have Daliyah disqualified and no longer running track for the league before she can say hello to Mickey Mouse after the finals.

As we enter the hotel's front entrance, the front desk clerk calls us over. I'd rather gobble up those fresh cookies sitting on the table next to the check-in counter. And they have lemonade.

"Are you Monica James?" the front desk clerk asks.

"Who is asking?" my mother answers, stepping in front of me.

"I saw the article they had in the paper talking about your race today."

"I'm Cynthia James, her mother. Is there a problem?"

The clerk comes around to the front of the counter and I'm frozen for a moment. What is going on?

"The athletic trainer at the meet today brought your bracelet back. As a matter of fact, he walked in thirty seconds after you dashed out." She hands me the bracelet. Then, without giving it a second thought, I give her the biggest hug. The Jaws of Life couldn't pry me off her.

"Monica, you are scaring the woman," my mother advises while pulling me away.

"Ms..." I look at her nametag, "Ms. Tisdale, you made my day!"

"I see," Ms. Tisdale smooths out her uniform. "Glad I brought a smile to your cute face. You looked pitiful earlier."

"I lost my race," I snap the bracelet back around my wrist.

"There's next season," Ms. Tisdale encourages me.

"Not with Miss Monica, ma'am. She is determined to win every race, so losses aren't accepted," Mom interjects. "Nevertheless, I'm glad you are repeating what I already told her. She's only eleven."

"Soon to be twelve," I stress.

"She'll be twelve next month."

"Only eleven and three-quarters? You have plenty of time to redeem yourself. But, I'm glad the bracelet cheered you up," Ms. Tisdale beams.

"Sure did! Thanks!" As she walks away, I start doing the MC Hammer dance on the way to the elevator. To add to my joy, I begin to sing, "I got my bracelet. I got my bracelet. Reunited, and it feels so good! On my wrist like you know you should. Where would I be if …"

"Monica, I love you, but get on this elevator!" My mother points me in the direction I need to be heading.

Being an obedient child, I dance my way onto the elevator.

"Baby, maybe this is a sign," my mom suggests while pushing the button for our floor.

As much as I want to respond, I'm still unsure of what I want to happen between D and I. After dinner, my mind is still racing. Sometimes when I can't talk to anyone or whoever I need to talk to doesn't seem to be hearing me, I have to tell Diana, my diary, everything (stresses and blessings). Yes, I named my diary Diana. No one really wants to say Dear Diary and the next best name is Diana. DIA-RY, DIA-NA . . . get it?

> *Dear Diana,*
>
> *Losing the bracelet D gave me made me lose my mind today. Straight trippin'. When I miraculously got it back, my mom said it was a sign. It just made me wonder if D and I could return to how we used to be if we don't work out. I have seen it in the movies and at school. Kids our age don't stay together. Me and my friends have boyfriends every other month. My longest relationship in fifth grade lasted three months. It was easy to hide since I only saw the boy at school. Nevertheless, I got tired of him.*

D is my homie and I don't want to lose my friend, my best friend, over a kiss and deciding to be his girlfriend. I can now see what Sharise and Tia see in him, but what if being his girlfriend jacks that up?

*If my father knows we are going out, the whole way we chill will change. I don't care what Mom says. Daddy is not going to be cool with this! My daddy doesn't care if he accidentally brushes my shoulder, the boy will wake up with one less toe. You know he likes to remind **everyone**, "My name ain't Lawrence for no reason. I run the **law** in everything!" D can't lose a toe, and I can't lose being able to kick it with my homie. I value our friendship too much!*

CHAPTER 6

THE KISS

Donovan Brown

My mind keeps going back to when I finally decided to surprise MJ with the braided bracelet. She had been going on and on about it before we went to Chuck-E-Cheese. She was determined to double her tickets by getting mine. She was overly confident, which caused her to talk more junk than a little bit. It also made her look good but I didn't let that distract me from killin' every game. When she started smelling herself, she wanted the last battle to be hoops. I don't know why. She knows basketball was, and still is, my sport. She can do her thing, too, but my skillz are mad dope.

I killed her confidence, quieted her noise and she went pouting to the van. Even my mom and Aunt Cynthia clowned her. It was too funny. While riding home, she wouldn't even sit by me or talk to me. Finally, I had to man up and sit next to the fire simmering. I knew the bracelet was the water to cool her down. Yeah, your boy definitely saw her cheesing in the window.

She wanted to stay mad, but I knew I got her. Daddy's advice definitely worked. I watched how she lit up when she talked about that bracelet, so I had already planned to get it for her whether I won the battle or not. I had some tickets I brought from home, so I'd have a way to get them.

You're probably wondering why I didn't let her win knowing I had enough tickets. It isn't our style to let anyone win. You don't produce champions by punking out or not competing.

I digress.

When I went in for the kiss, it just felt right. MJ looked *fine*. The kiss felt like it did in my dreams. I just wish the ending was the same with her becoming my girl. The way she reacted tells me that might not happen.

Again, I just knew we would be boyfriend and girlfriend after that moment, but her brother came and busted up the mood. Before I rushed into the house, I tried to say bye, but she was staring out of the window again. I wasn't sure if I crossed the line or if she didn't like it. I didn't know what to think. Maybe I do know what to think because she didn't pull away immediately.

Besides being clueless about how she felt, it didn't help that we didn't have a James and Browns' meet-up for at least three weeks. Our schedules were crazy due to family vacations and sports.

Hanging out with my boy, Lou, I'm still trippin' over Monica's reaction to the kiss. A part of me doesn't even want to bring this up to Lou. I can hear him bragging on how he knew I liked Monica. Yet, he seems to be a little more experienced with girls so maybe he can tell me what Monica is thinking. But he isn't the best at dealing with girls.

Dang, I must really be desperate if I'm turning to Lou for advice.

Naw, I can't do it.

"D, what's up with you, dog?" asks Lou, who notices I'm not barking my usual trash talk during the video game. On top of him noticing something is up with me, I feel like all the miniature statues on my   and my brother's trophies are telling me to speak up. Then the most comfortable couch my mom gave to us when they bought a new one for the family room is all of the sudden uncomfortable. The temperature of the room is hot and clammy so I turn the ceiling fan on.

"What?" I ask to avoid telling all my business. Despite the fan blowing a cool breeze, I start fanning myself, attempting to distract myself from the obvious truth that I'm bugging.

"You seem down and how are you hot?" He isn't letting up.

"I'm good, dog," I lie then blow out frustration.

"You frontin'. I beat you three times in a row, and you don't have anything to say about it? That never happens." He looks me up and down like he is searching for the truth then he gets up and turns off the game.

"Yooo, what did you do that for?" I protest.

"What is your problem, dog?" He lets the remote fall to the carpeted floor.

As much as I don't trust how this moment of truth will unfold, I breathe out another sigh of relief because I can finally get this mess off my chest. After getting up to close the door with a life size poster of Michael Jordan on the back, I whisper, "You have to keep your mouth shut about this. And I ain't tryin' to hear, I told you so."

"Ummmm, why are you whispering?" Lou doesn't whisper well at all and he is watching me like I'm straight trippin'. I know I look crazy but he doesn't understand how important getting this news off my chest is to me.

"Shhhhhhh. You know my parents got hearing better than dogs, man. Don't play me." I look at the door like my parents or brother can walk in at any moment.

"What is up? Do I need to knock someone out?" he lowers his voice, not breaking eye contact with me.

"Naw, man. It ain't like that," I breathe out another sigh of relief but take my time trying to figure out how to tell him what I need to say.

"Um, you going to spill it today?" He throws his hands up in frustration.

"Chill out. I… ummmmm," I begin and stall as I look toward the door again. I thought I heard Nick trying to come in, then I realize I'm just paranoid. If he gets wind of this, I will have to kick his butt every day. Lou will also rag me 'til no end but I don't have to live with him.

"What is the deal, man? Got me over here sweating!" Lou panics. "You what?" He shakes some nerves back into me.

"I, ummmmmmm, I kissed MJ."

"Michael Jackson or Michael Jordan?" He looks dumbfounded. "Either way, why wasn't I there to witness this?"

"Sometimes I swear, Lou," I mush his head. "*Oh my gosh*, dude, *MJ* is Monica."

"I know, fool! Gotta bust a jokey joke! You over here sweating bullets! Why you trippin'? It's 'bout dang time!" he shouts and gives me dap.

"Shut up, Lou!" I say, but still give him dap as I blush at the memory.

"Yo, I'm sorry." He beams then lowers his voice, "Are her lips as soft as they look?"

"Heck yeah!" I realize I'm loud like him then whisper, "Heck yeah." We dap each other up again.

"I knew it!" He holds his hands up to apologize for what I told him not to do. "I know you said not to rag you, but you have been frontin' like she ain't fine! If you never admitted it, I would question your intelligence." As much as I want to give him an explanation or rag him back for calling me stupid, which technically he is right, I tell him play by play how it went down. The look on Lou's face is pure excitement and I have to keep reminding him to keep his voice down.

Then all of the sudden he is confused. "I still don't understand why you trippin'. You said the kiss was good. Was your breath stank?" He looks like he is going down a list.

I let him know that I popped a Tic Tac in my mouth so I know my breath wasn't a problem. Then he had the nerve to ask if I tried to tongue kiss her, which to me is swapping spit. He says I would like it, but it sounds disgusting to me. Flabbergasted, he is wondering how I jacked it up by striking out after I finally get the nerve to step up to the plate. I have to remind him I made it to first base, but he reiterates I didn't walk away from that kiss with MJ being my girl.

Beyond being frustrated, I again ask Lou what I need to do. Lou says I just need to chill out. I could have freaked her out. I never told MJ I liked her. I mean I sorta did that day in the woods, but I couldn't get my words together so she didn't understand what I was trying to say. I definitely don't know if she likes me, so that kiss could have her buggin'. Maybe she is feeling me but she's just scared. She did kiss me back.

Lou rags me again for not making my move sooner. How can I have a best friend who is a *fine* girl who I don't use to my advantage to play games that require her to give me CPR? He doesn't understand what being a gentleman is all about. If he can play, flirt, kiss, and touch girls' butts all day, every day, he will and never get tired of it. He is what girls call a playa, which will never be me.

My dad says he will eventually get played or just played out.

With our schedules, our next James and Brown meet-up is a week later. Dinner is at my house, which always leads to video games in the playroom. I haven't said much to her since they got here and she hasn't said anything to me, either. But I can't miss this opportunity to see what she's thinking. I need to know if she likes me the way I like her.

When I see her head to the playroom, I follow her. Thankfully, our brothers haven't made it in here yet, so I have the perfect opportunity to talk to her without them all in our business. She's sitting on the couch, holding the remote control and waiting for me to put in a video game. I put in Tecmo Bowl and I sit down next to her, taking a deep breath before I speak.

"So, how have you been?" I hesitantly ask.

She won't look at me for some reason and it's making me nervous looking around the room with walls covered with posters of sports all-stars, rappers and singers.

My brother and I both have a desk in opposite corners of the room where we do homework. I notice for the first time there is a picture of MJ and I framed over my desk along with a few others. Nevertheless, that picture of us as five-year-olds smiling at the camera on the beach draws my attention.

After a long pause, she replies, "I've been okay. You know I lost the semifinals to Daliyah." She's focusing on the screen more than me, but I don't let that stop me. We have to have this conversation.

"You will get her next summer." I know MJ. She loves winning and she'll do everything she can in the off season to make sure she's ready to win next summer. That's one of the things I love about her. She just doesn't give up.

"D, how did I go from finishing in the top four to not even finishing the race?" she almost whines and I wonder if I need to have this conversation about us later. "And I'm better than her," she adds.

Knowing she needs to get it all out, I decide our conversation about the kiss can wait. "True that," I agree because it's the truth. MJ is the best at track and rarely loses. "I get it."

After another long pause, she says, "I can't prove it, but I think she elbowed me."

Daliyah and MJ had a rivalry that went back for years. Well, more like a one-sided rivalry since MJ won most of the races when they met on the track.

I'd watched Daliyah a few times after MJ beat her in a race and could tell she was jealous, but was she angry enough to cheat? I wasn't sure but if MJ said she thinks something happened, I believe her. She's not the type to look for an excuse to justify losing.

"Word?" I don't understand why Daliyah would stoop that low. By now, I turn and face her, hoping she will look up at me and see that I'm still the same D. I don't like how she is coming off guarded. Our friendship can't turn into this.

"Word," MJ replies. "When my mom finally brought it up to Coach Baker, he said there was nothing they could do. No one was recording that day."

I sighed deeply, running my right hand over my waves to remain calm. This was messed up but there is more that can be done. "MJ, someone is always recording."

"I know but my parents told me to let it go!" She is almost yelling now.

"When have you have ever just let it go because someone said so and you knew better?" I urge her while giving her the green light she needed to right a wrong. Monica has a gift at knowing when something isn't right, and she'll keep ripping away at the issue until she finds out the truth.

Once, she started noticing TJ was very quiet as they rode the bus home. He would eat everything once they got in the house. Some would use the excuse he was a growing boy, but Monica knew something was up. After about three days of him not being himself, she went to her parents about it. TJ played it off like it was nothing.

One day she convinced her teacher to let her go to the cafeteria during his lunch and witnessed her brother being forced to give his food to a punk bully. As much as she wanted to fight his battle, she knew that would only make TJ look like a sucker, so she decided to teach him how to stand up for himself.

At home, she had a talk with TJ and they had a "training session." Before he went to school the next day, he felt like he was Mike Tyson. His boosted confidence gave him the courage to sucker punch the bully in the face, causing all the boys on the bus to hype him up the whole ride home. He was hailed a hero because his sister wouldn't let it go when she knew there was something wrong.

"If you say she hit you, I believe you. Your intuition is never wrong." She finally makes eye contact then nods her head in agreement. There is this weird silence so I decide to say what I have been wanting to know for weeks. "Monica, I need to know something," I scoot closer to her.

"What's up," she looks me up and down warily.

"How do you feel about our kiss? Do you know how long I wanted to do that?" I pause but don't expect an answer. "I want you to be my girlfriend." It feels like a weight has been lifted from my shoulders until she responds.

"D, you know Daddy A.K.A. Lawrence B.K.A The Law?"

So she is scared of how her dad will react, but she still didn't answer my question. Did she like the kiss as much as I did?

"I asked you if you liked the kiss and you bring up your pops?" I look away. I have a feeling what she is about to say next. This is going to break my heart if she rejects me.

"D, I," she pauses then says softly, "I loved the kiss. My first kiss and it was with you." She looks up at me. Before my soul can get happy, she shatters my hope, "But we can't. You know my dad will trip. Don't be mad."

She then admits that Tia and Sharise had a feeling I was digging her and I let her know that Lou suspected it too and wondered why I took so long to approach her. Her dad has nothing to do with it. I just didn't want to mess it up.

Surprisingly, she didn't realize she had feelings for me until the day of the kiss. Ever since that day, she couldn't stop thinking of me but also how this is a crazy situation that her father would not approve of.

After she is done spilling her guts about her emotions playing tug-a-war, I just want to kiss away her fears. I'm mad but I cannot deny I miss her and I want her to be my girlfriend. I believe that somehow her pops will remember who I am, his godson who's always been a stand-up dude. MJ doesn't agree and doesn't understand my frustration.

"How would you feel if someone you really liked shot you down?"

"Being that you are my best friend, I would hope he... you... would not trip. Be patient with me. So much would change if we started going steady. We should just forget about how we feel about each other, you know?"

How does she expect me to forget about how I feel? She is acting like my feelings are a light switch or something didn't grow from a kiss, our first kiss. She has been on my heart and mind since I was ten.   She is more than just a crush. I can't just stop digging this girl who is supposed to be my girl.

I look up and see her looking down at the floor. She can't even look me in the eyes again. She is lying to herself if she thinks we can just forget about how we feel.

I try to convince her that we can keep it quiet between us until we figure out how to tell her father. She shocks me with the truth that my mom and her mom, Mrs. Cynthia, already knew I always felt something deeper for MJ. She also told her mom about the kiss. *What the heck?* Bump all that. I know she doesn't want to be my girl now, but I need another kiss.

"Since you liked the kiss," I grin and she immediately starts blushing causing a chain reaction. I can't stop blushing, either. She is so *fine,* beautiful.

She scoots a little closer to me. We both check our breath and it is cool, giving us the green light to repeat that moment from weeks ago. I hear cheers from guys on my posters and trophies. The second time is even sweeter because MJ has on cherry lip gloss. A part of me doesn't care if our parents walk in.

As much as I want to tell her she is wrong, I know she is right about everything. Being alone like we are now will completely go out of the window if Mr. James found out about us. How will I deal with seeing her every day knowing we can't be together?

I enjoy the kiss and promise myself it won't be our last. It hurts, but I refuse to lose her. I don't care how long it takes and I refuse to give up.

One day, MJ will be my girlfriend.

POETIC INTERMISSION

Donovan Brown

This is More Than a Crush

Have you ever fallen in love with your best friend?
Finally have the nerve to ask,
"Check yes or no,"
after the glow of her lips pressed against yours?
Better than the dreams, better than imagining.
Real as my heart beats for her.
Opened the door to more or so I had hoped.
Yet, my dreams are shattered, my heart is broken.
She wants to pretend like love doesn't exist.
Fire isn't ignited when our hands touch.
Just to look into her eyes warms
that place in my heart aching for her.
I will wait for her.
Another girl, no other girl is like her.
I will turn my world upside down to let her back in
if she just opens her heart, checks yes.
No, there is no escaping this feeling.
My pops says I'm too young to handle.
Cradling it like a newborn.
Careful not to hold too tight.
I heard what you let go will come back.
Just hope that tale is proven fact over myth.
Until then…

CHAPTER 7

LET THE GAMES BEGIN

Donovan Brown

As amped as I am to be in junior high, two things *suck*: I can't play sports like I used to and can't rock MJ on my arm. Usually, I play three sports a year, but my parents want to see how well I balance six classes with six different teachers and my core classes are all honors.

Then there is MJ. My best friend, the girl I love but can't be with. It doesn't help that I will see her more than ever since we are attending the same school. Now I heard there are a lot of fly honeys in junior high, but I would rather be with MJ.

Confessing a brotha's emotions has me feelin' her more. *It sucks.*   I don't know why she is making this so difficult, anyway. Seriously, I don't care about our parents knowing anymore, especially her dad.

I asked if we could still kiss sometimes and thought she would take me up on my offer. She never lived up to her end of the bargain. In a way, I get it.

But let's be real, it's not just kissing when you are kissing the girl you love.

Yes, I love this girl. Lou keeps saying I'm too young for love but what else can I call it when she is always on my mind? "All I Do is Think of You" is our unofficial theme song. She doesn't know. Another one has the lyrics, "I only think of you on two occasions. That's day and night." Yes, my boys have witnessed me more than once belting out a R&B love song out of tune when I put Boys II Men or Jodeci in my Walkman. Lou is the only one who knows I'm singing about MJ.

As my dad and I are waiting at the bus stop on the first day of school, I notice a new kid just standing there. "Dad, who's that?"

He looks up from his paper. "I saw the moving truck over the weekend. Last name is Johnson. I don't remember the first name."

"You met them?"

"Out during my morning run, I introduced myself to the dad and his son. The boy is in your grade. Dad is in the Air Force, so they got stationed here. Seems real cool. You know your mom will have them over for dinner one day soon."

"Yeap, Mrs. Welcoming Committee."

"You gonna just sit in the car or go introduce yourself?"

After telling my dad bye and I love him, I get out of the car and walk toward the new kid. "What up?"

"What up?" says the new guy.

"Donovan Brown." I dap him up.

"Will Johnson."

Then there's an awkward silence as I look back at my dad, wondering what to say next.

"You always ride with your pops to the bus stop?"

"It's a neighborhood thing to have at least one adult out here. Making sure no strange people try to pick us up. The sun isn't up yet."

"Why we gotta catch the bus so early? It is killing my sleep game."

"I know but we get out earlier," I reason.

"I guess that's a plus," he shrugs.

I confirm what my dad says about us being in the same grade. We find out we are both ballers. I share how I used to do soccer, basketball, and track. My mom told me I might be able to try out for basketball this fall and track if I keep my grades up. I wish I could still play AAU ball, but she said maybe next year. He says that his parents are being strict about him playing sports, too, since he has a heavy course load as well. He considers himself an all-star athlete just like I do. Unlike me, he played football on both sides of the field. After bragging about his stats in each sport, he stands like a rapper posing for a photo shoot with his arms crossing his chest.

"You got it like that?"

"Yes, sir! Ain't trying to brag but don't know where my team will be this year without me."

I can dig his confidence, but I will admit it comes off a little cocky. Still this dude seems pretty cool despite the fact that he wants to challenge my reign as the fastest homie on the block. If the bus wasn't rolling up, we would definitely race. We vow to race after school today.

He's a betting dude, but I don't wager when I'm not sure about my odds. Sizing him up and down, I'm not confident if I will keep my title. I don't have to prove anything to him, but I definitely ain't trying to lose any money or give up something else of value. So I bet that beating him is all the bragging rights I need.

"Yo, who is this lame cat talking all this noise?" shouts Lou as he finally makes it to the bus stop. He lives right in front of the bus stop so sometimes he waits until the last minute to come out of the house.

"This is Will Johnson. He's from?"

"Jacksonville, FL. And this lame cat will dust both of y'all in a race."

"I'll let you and D handle that. I haven't beat him since third grade."

"Fastest dude on the block, and I don't plan on giving up that title," I pat myself on the chest.

"Trying to get your dude to place a bet. What's your name?" Will inquires.

"Lou Stevens. Naw, D very rarely takes bets, especially when it comes to women."

"Don't tell me you a punk with the ladies, Donovan, or can I call you, D?" clowns Will.

I wave to my dad in the car before getting on the bus.

"Homie, we don't know you so it is Donovan," Lou retorts.

Will holds both of his hands up.

"He's right. But what you not going to do is play me. Lou knows I don't have to use game. I'm too fly to use game."

"Cocky?" Will asks.

"Confident I can get any girl I want," I boast.

"Any girl?" mocks Lou. I just stare at him to shut up. He knows what went down between MJ and me. He blames me for her turning me down. Said I took too long. According to Monica, I didn't take long enough. She is fighting the awkwardness of calling her best friend her boyfriend. Then you can't ignore how her father feels about her even having a boyfriend. *But it is me.* How can he deny me?

"I guess I will eventually find out what the inside joke is," Will sneers.

Lou starts laughing then chills out to spare my heartache and to prevent a quick punch to the chest.

On the bus ride to school, you would never know it is too early for anyone to be up. It isn't loud and rowdy but there is a quiet excitement among the young bucks who are embarking on their first day of junior high. Some sit alone looking nervous. Others I can tell know each other from the neighborhood or elementary school. There are also kids hyping each other's outfits, fresh cuts, and hairstyles.

Also, I find out what else makes Will cool. We have the same favorite college football team, Florida State. Because Florida State sucks in basketball, we both love Duke for college basketball. When it comes to the pros, we are both fans of the Chicago Bulls and San Francisco 49ers. He's in all honors classes, so I will get to see another familiar face in the crowd.

What isn't cool about being in honors classes, I heard, is not seeing enough faces like mine. My cousin said there are plenty of females, but he would be maybe the fifth Black dude in a class of twenty-five.

Not cool.

You would think I would be used to being around fewer people who look like me in the classroom. It never gets old. As much as Lou likes to act stupid, he knows his parents don't play with him about his grades. Having slack grades or behavior has never been accepted by my family or anyone in our circle. Being on the honor roll is like breathing, but it never ceases to amaze me when other people are shocked Black boys can have manners, be intelligent, and ball.

My parents understand their sons are true athletes, and they refuse to allow us to be just that. So as a result, I can't participate in sports this fall. I told them I could handle it. My pops told me to focus on the books, and we can go from there. It is what it is, but it still sucks.

As we follow the directions of one of the faculty members after getting off the bus, we find ourselves in the gym looking at all the other students waiting to be released to their homeroom. Thank goodness we are not separated into grade levels or classes like elementary school.

Once Will, Lou, and I strut into the gym, we instantly noticed the amount of hotties in the building. Since MJ wants to play games, I will grab another girl, maybe even an eighth grader. I've heard I look mature for my age.

Some would say I'm being immature because I'm willing to make a point to MJ versus just waiting for her. Wouldn't I look like a chump waiting while all these dudes are stepping to her? I can't handle that when she should be *my* girl. I prayed to God she will see no other dude is like me because there is no doubt other dudes will step to her.

"Hey, lover boy," I hear an unfamiliar voice call out from the top of the bleachers as we are directed to the next row of available seats.

"Who is that?" exclaims Lou.

"All I know is she is fine," whispers Will.

I look up to see who is speaking, confirming what my eyes are now seeing.

"Yes, I'm talking to you. What grade are you in?" she flirts.

I clear my throat to make my voice deep, "Seventh."

"Cute," she compliments.

She looks very familiar. "Thanks. What's your name?"

"Daliyah Jennings. I would come down there to get a closer look, but I heard the teachers are really strict about you moving around. What's your name?"

"Donovan Brown." *This is MJ's archrival trying to holla at me.*

"You look very familiar, Donovan Brown."

Should I play like I don't know who she is? I don't know what happened over the summer but she is fine. She is really fine, but MJ would kill me if I kicked game to the enemy.

I hear my dad in my head, "*You're a young man of integrity.*"

"Now I remember. You're like best friends with Monique," Daliyah smirks.

"Her name is Monica," I correct her but I wanted to add *the one who has been beating you for years.* I don't believe in going back and forth with a girl I barely know. Besides, she would throw her win this summer over MJ in my face. A win she had to cheat to earn. She's the enemy who won Nationals because there was no evidence to prove she literally strong-armed her way to the finish line.

I will leave it alone.

"Monica, Monique, it sounds the same. I know she is lame for saying you were just a friend," she flirts.

"And she says he's just a friend," her friends sing.

"Oh, baby, you!" Lou chimes in singing loudly, "got what I need!"

"Shut up," I mush him on the head.

"That is my joint, D!" he wops to the imaginary song playing in his head.

"Donovan, you got what I need so let me get those digits please," Daliyah raps to me.

"Naw, I'm good." I turn around to Will who looks confused and agitated.

"Yo, are you blind?" Will questions. "She is fine!"

"I'll fill you in later," I say out of earshot.

"All I know is Monica won't have it. She is fine but Monica would kill you," Lou fails at an attempt to whisper.

"Yo, Lou, shut up!" I mouth.

"I think you need new friends, Donovan, so here is my number." Daliyah writes it down on a piece of paper and passes it down through her friends. As her friends attempt to hand me the number, I keep my eyes looking forward. Let word get to MJ that I took Daliyah's number and that will lock me out of her heart for life.

Will snatches it. "I got you, Daliyah. My boy is shy."

As much as I want to check Will, I'm captivated by Monica who is walking into the gym with pink overalls and matching high top sneakers

"Meet Monica," Lou confirms, nodding his head in her direction.

"Oh, this is the Monica Daliyah was talking smack about. I see Daliyah has some competition," Will resounds.

"Ain't nobody competing for D," Lou heckles.

I shoot Lou a look that I hope shuts him up.

"What? Tell me I'm lying. Someone" he pauses and throws his hands up. "I will shut up now."

"Hold up? Why isn't Monica your girl?" Will demands.

I have to give him the same spill I used to give Lou. I get the same reaction, but am shocked when I let something go down I would never let Lou do.

"So, you don't mind if I holla at her?" Will doesn't even notice me and Lou's silent conversation.

He's mesmerized by my girl while Lou is urging me to deny Will his request. I go against every bubble in my gut with a straight face. While lying to myself, I say, "I'll hook you up, and maybe I'll hook myself up with that fly chick who came in with MJ. She's new."

"What about Daliyah?" Will hints.

"What about her? You have her number."

"Technically, it is for you. Hold up! You ever been in MJ's room?" Will marvels.

"Yeah," I confirm nonchalantly.

"Y'all never played doctor or house?" Will just won't quit.

"That's what I said," Lou echoes. "Finally, somebody is feeling me on this!"

"Y'all are real wack right now." I shake my head.

"You wack! She is fine. She isn't banging like Daliyah up there and her crew, but she is fine!" Will declares.

"There is more to her than just being fine." I look in her direction, making sure I don't stare. The new haircut makes it hard to focus. Her bangs and picture perfect bob hugs her face beautifully. "She's a good girl, so I will introduce y'all two." I cross my fingers it won't work between her and Will. Lou just shakes his head, ashamed.

I found out during orientation MJ and I have no classes together this year, which sucks. When her mom found out, she said it would keep us both focused. I guess she is right, but I will see her at recess. Will, Lou, and I compared our schedules on the bus and saw Will and I have most classes together. Lou doesn't have homeroom with us along with PE. He has art and I know he will use that class to mack girls.

After lunch, Lou, Will, and I head out for recess, which I think is super cool. In elementary school, we had a scheduled time that the teacher would take us out. In middle school, we are free to go out as soon as we finish our lunch. Super dope!

When we get outside, we see people playing basketball and football. Some girls are watching the guys, and some are doing their own thing like jumping Double Dutch.

I immediately spot MJ in the Double Dutch crew with her new friend. Her name is Nicole Myers but everyone calls her Nikki. I caught her giving me the eye in class several times today. Will claims she was giving *him* the eye. However, Will sits right next to me, so he said it is possible. Also, I had to remind him he wants MJ, so we agree to disagree while he bet me Nicole is next.

All three of us look around the blacktop trying to figure out what we want to do. Despite Will and I wanting to play either basketball or football,

Lou convinces us we don't want to get funky today while macking the honeys. I'm not trying to mack anybody since I can't be with MJ. Yeah, I mentioned Nicole but I ain't really serious.

Will beckons me to introduce him to MJ. We wait for MJ to finish her turn jumping then she walks over with Nicole.

"What's up, fellas?" MJ grins taking the scrunchie out of her hair she was using to put it up while she jumped. It effortlessly falls into place, taking my breath away. I forget to breathe for a second.

"Hey, MJ. I mean, Monica." I'm the only one who calls her MJ. Lou even understands not to utter that nickname. "You know Lou, and this is Will. He moved right down the street."

"What's up, Lou? Will, nice to meet you." MJ then turns to the new girl. "This is Nicole. She's new to the neighborhood, too."

We discuss our classes and how we believe our teachers are straight trippin' on the first day of school.

"And why is Daliyah here? I gotta be in class with her and run on the same team as her. " I guess she plans on going out for track this spring.

"I ran into her this morning," I mention.

"Yeah, I heard she gave you them digits," MJ gave me a look that could kill.

"Will took her number," Lou attempts to help a brother out. "He doesn't know the history."

"I didn't know this morning but now I know. Enemies, huh?" Will laughs. "I asked Donovan to introduce you and me. Hard to believe he hasn't scooped you up yet," Will flirts.

"We were actually talking about meeting at the movies this weekend and were hoping," struggling through my words, I don't realize someone is coming to interrupt this sorry excuse of a love connection.

"Donovan, there you are! I've been looking for you," Daliyah sings as she approaches. "Monique, hey, girl!"

"I told you," I retort.

"I got this, D." She turns to Daliyah. "Don't play stupid. You know my name is Monica. The one who came in first to your second place," Monica fires back.

"Oh but this summer someone had a mishap over the hurdle," Daliyah cackles. "Awe, what a tragedy." She pretends to pout then it quickly turns into a smirk.

"You know exactly why I didn't win that race," Monica steps to her forgetting we don't entertain riff raff.

"I heard you tried to get the officials to investigate. No such luck with finding evidence," Daliyah chirps up.

"Why are you over here?" I hiss, attempting to divert Daliyah's attention. Also, looking around to ensure none of the teachers notice what could potentially go down. Seriously, what is she up to?

"I wanted to make sure Will gave you my number. We should hang out Saturday night."

"Yo, he already has a date, Daliyah, so chill out," Lou intervenes. I need him to be quiet. The last thing I need Daliyah to know is my plans for the weekend. Sumter doesn't have a lot of movie theaters so it won't be hard to stalk us.

"With who?" both Daliyah and MJ beckon.

"Before we were interrupted, we were trying to ask you and Nicole if you wanted to go to the movies," Will steps in front of Daliyah, facing MJ.

"Looks like someone already has plans, Dally, so step," emphasizes Nicole. Nicole has some spunk about her.

"It is—" Daliyah attempts to correct her.

"You don't know how to pronounce anyone's name correctly so skiddaddle, be gone," MJ interjects.

"I will see you around, Big D." Daliyah waves goodbye to me as she slowly walks away backward.

"Yoooo, did she just give you a new nickname?" Lou heckles while looking at MJ. "I felt violated and that stuff usually turns me on."

"Shut up, Lou!" MJ and I both yell.

In an effort to get back to his mission, Will shifts the subject to getting to know MJ. She lifts up that one infamous eyebrow at Will, then at me.

"Yeah, so Monica, what are you doing this Saturday?" I ask.

Monica looks at me weirdly. I don't know the last time I called her Monica. Granted, it was twice in this conversation but it is still rare.

"This Saturday?" MJ still gives us an incredulous look. She's hot when she's happy, mad, sad, and salty. "What's going on?" she questions.

"Will and I are going to the movies. Maybe you and Nicole can join us like a double date, you know?"

"Who is dating who?" she looks back and forth between Will and I then her and Nicole.

"You are too fine," Will interrupts waltzing up to her grabbing her hand. "I have to get to know you. Donovan is a fool for just being a homie. You too pretty not to be more. I'm down."

MJ looks confused and is probably wondering why I didn't tell him I *did* holla at her. She must have forgotten she told me to forget about how I feel about her. She knows I can't, so I'm shocking her by making her eat her own words.

Reluctantly, she and Nicole agree to meet us there right before the bell rings, sending us back to class. Before dashing to class, she reminds me we need to pick a theater because we have three of them. I shout to her back we are going to Cinema Twin, and she signals with a quick thumbs up while I notice Daliyah all in our conversation. After they were out of earshot, Lou gives me that look again letting a brother know I'm stupid for not being honest with Will about my feelings for MJ.

Something good may come out of this, like MJ realizing she can't forget how she feels about me. She can't act like what we share isn't real. Maybe she will realize she doesn't want anyone else to have me. It's worth a try, right?

After we get home from school, Lou gets Will to agree to race later because we've got some business to handle. He has been itching to check me on my bright idea since I agreed to this *foolishness*, in his words.

"You really going to go through with this? This double date debacle?" Lou badgers.

"Using your big words. It won't even go down like that. MJ said she didn't want me, so why not?"

"Because you still want her! And she still wants you. How didn't you see that today?"

I had no response.

"So, you saw it too and you're still going through with this? You call me the stupid one, and you're over here playing cupid with your woman and some dude you just met. *Debacle!*"

"MJ ain't gonna be feeling him like that."

"So, you set up ol' dude to fail? He's one cocky dude who is aggravating, but you didn't have to introduce him to Monica. If he all that, he would have macked her himself. Oh, here's a bright idea: *introduce him to someone else!* And you're supposed to be the smart one!"

"Tell me how you really feel." I shake my head in disgust but he is technically right.

"He doesn't know you like I know you. He hasn't seen your nose wide open since forever over this girl. The more I think about it, the more I see you had me fooled for a minute, too. When you finally admitted you been feeling her and *kissed* her, I realized the signs were always there. I hope this doesn't blow up your spot."

"I got this! Chill out, homes. We gotta focus on this homework." I walk away, hoping Lou isn't right.

CHAPTER 8

STUCK IN THE MIDDLE

Monica James

Attending the same junior high as D is doing exactly what I had a feeling would happen. The opposite of what my mom promised and what I didn't want to happen. My mom tried to calm my nerves by assuring me everything will be alright, but I can't ignore the kiss. I can't forget my newly discovered feelings for D. Tia and Sharise would go crazy while slapping me over the phone line. I could hear them now.

"You straight trippin' to let go of Don!" Tia would scold.

"You must have fell and bumped your head! What in the world, Monica?" Sharise would lecture.

Although I don't have my two former best friends to scold me about turning D down, I'm elated to have a new potential best friend who is going on a double date with me and D but as D's date. What is really going on in the world?

Nicole Meyers and I met on the bus ride to school today. She loves doing her nails, listens to all types of music, and enjoys competing and watching sports like me. She is the twin version of me, which is super dope crazy cool. Tia and Sharise were my homies but it would suck when they would get all prissy or mad when they broke a nail.

Despite us being super cool already, what is not cool is I can't be honest about how I really feel about D and what could be a disastrous date. This has to be the worse first day of school ever.

Will is cute and all but I'm not feeling him and his cockiness. D's friends never tried to holla at me, which I now know why. When I told him to forget we have feelings for each other, that wasn't an invitation for him to play Love Connection with me and his homies. Before I knew I had feelings for D, I would never *holla* at his friends.

I expected D to be with other girls *except* Daliyah Jennings. I heard sometimes boys don't get it, which is why you have to spell things out to them. Forgetting how you feel about me doesn't give you the green light to hook me up.

As a first day of school tradition, my mom makes it home earlier than usual after she leaves school. It doesn't matter if she comes home early or late, she always asks about my brother's and my day. Since he is in elementary school, he is at the after school program where my dad will pick him up.

After my mother asks about school, I tell her I believe it is already too hard, but she isn't hearing it. Then she reminds me I'm not allowed to have any C's.

I had to tell her about Nicole since I want us to go to the movies Saturday. I leave out D and Will joining us but tell her I think D likes Nicole, how Daliyah gave D her number, and how Daliyah admitted without saying she is the reason why I fell over in the semifinals race.

"Donovan can't find other girls cute?" First, she addresses my frustration with D asking out Nicole.

"I don't know. We just decided a few weeks ago not to go steady. Now he is checking out another girl who is like my homegirl."

After taking out some grapes and the Kool-Aid pitcher, I slam the fridge door.

"Please don't tear up my appliances."

"I didn't mean to slam it. It's just… frustrating." I go into the cabinet to get a glass to pour my Kool-Aid.

"You being Miss Social Butterfly and as cute as D is, it is bound to happen. I'm so glad y'all don't have any classes together this year. You can't let this situation distract you."

"Mom, you know I'm serious about my work." I go over to the sink to wash off the grapes.

"I know, baby, but every pre-teen goes through the big change. Some excel academically and others bomb out while getting too involved with drama or anything else that has nothing to do with school. Just know you don't have an option to be average. Do we need to sit down and have a talk with the Jennings's family?"

"Mom, now you know they believe Daliyah doesn't do anything wrong. You know she laughed that there is no evidence about her side swiping me at the race?" I finally sit down at the table.

"She seems to know how to push your buttons."

I just take a large gulp from my glass of red Kool-Aid.

My mom goes on to say that I can't allow myself to be bothered by Daliyah who unfortunately has the reigning title as the national champion of the 100 high hurdles in our age bracket. I have to remind her that proving she cheated will strip her of her title and being banned from running with the track league for at least three years. You know how humiliating that would be to be found out as a cheater and then told you can't compete? As a result, I can't let this go until justice is served.

Mom reminds me of what my grandmother likes to say, "What is done in the dark will always come out in the light." In other words, I don't need to focus on being Inspector Gadget. I need to focus on my books. I feel like she is trying to get me to focus because she doesn't believe my story, which I know isn't true. Maybe she sees "the bigger picture" as adults like to say.

"The school part is easy. Just a whole bunch of work." I push myself back from the table. "Did I make a mistake not to go steady with D?"

"Do you really like him or you just like him because other girls are liking him? Wait before you answer," she holds up her hand, "D is a likable guy, but you can't decide to be with him just because you can't stand to see him with anyone else. That is not fair. Nevertheless, if you really like him, go for it."

"Mom, it's too risky." I throw some grapes in my mouth.

"You are twelve, Monica. It's not like you are twenty-five and looking to marry him. You know I don't mind you having a little boyfriend if all y'all do is—"

"Study, hold hands, study, hug with space between us, study, and just blow kisses," I mock.

"You think I'm playing?" She snatches some of my grapes and chomps down like I don't already know she means what she says.

"I'm not testing you. Daddy said I'm too young for boyfriends."

Yes, my parents had the sex talk with me already. They started early teaching me about my body parts and who shouldn't touch you there, which is why I never played doctor or house like some of my other friends. My body is precious, so precious diamonds, roses, and rubies envy it, as my parents constantly remind me. They took it from the Bible and added a little bit to it. When I turned ten, they talked a little bit about sex. They saw they were grossing me out, so they have learned to give a little at a time.

Another talk came this summer after I turned twelve and I had to admit I kissed a boy, but I wouldn't tell my dad it was D. Surprisingly, he didn't insist on knowing who it was. I have a feeling my mom had something to do with him not prying. Also, my parents learned their little girl is still innocent. The kiss was special but it was just a kiss.

Nevertheless, Dad would flip if he found out I kissed D. He would flip D, kill him, resuscitate him, and then apologize to his parents for killing their firstborn. He likes D but isn't ready for me to have a boyfriend.

I tell Mom everything. She doesn't freak out and she doesn't just tell me what I want to hear. What I love most about her is how she listens. We are still working on Daddy.

A part of me wishes I could tell Nicole not to like D but if I'm honest… I can't have anyone telling me who I can and can't like. Let's be real, I don't even know if she likes him or if she just agreed to hang out with us.

After finishing homework earlier than I expected, I decided to give my new best friend a call.

"Tell me about this Donovan Brown," Nicole inquires

"Well, what do you want to k-know?" I stammer.

"First, I want to know why he isn't your boyfriend."

"Um, what?"

"You heard me. I wish my mom didn't pick me up early for my doctor's appointment. I was ready to give you the third degree on the bus ride home. I saw it all over your face."

"You crazy," I nervously laugh.

"Monica James or as he likes to say, MJ."

"Nicole Myers."

"That is my name so don't wear it out." I can see her twisting her neck.

"Uh, how do you know me so well?"

"The only one who was oblivious to you and Donovan's love affair is Will with his fine self."

"Wait, what?" I take the phone and stare at it like she can see me.

Nicole is into arrogant boys, which is why she is feeling Will. To her, cockiness is translated as intimidating confidence for some people. She admits that her and Will were giving each other the googly eyes in class so she was very confused when he asked me out versus her. Nevertheless, she likes that he is open to free game, which means if it didn't work out with me and him, he would move on to the next one. I don't understand talking to someone who used to talk to my homegirl, but she said only if it was an in and out visit. You can find out in the first phone call or meeting that you don't like someone.

Because I'm flabbergasted about this new discovery about her, she demands to know why D and I aren't boyfriend and girlfriend. I give Nicole a full breakdown of my history with Donovan, which includes him confessing his love for me after the kiss. While I explain, I'm questioning again if I made the right decision to just be friends or if I'm upset because he's moving on.

*

Saturday

"I really hope you confess your love to this brother. We don't need to make this date more awkward," Nicole says after we buy our tickets and walk in the movie theater.

"Whatever." I'm eyeing the movie posters going up the aisle to the concession stand of Cinema Twin.

"You want popcorn?" Nicole probes.

"Let the boys pay for it." I'm deciding what candy I'm going to let someone pay for.

"Will and D have money like that?" She is eyeing the prices.

"D gets a pretty nice allowance. Speaking of—"

"Sup, ladies. Monica, you are looking all that and a bag of Dorito chips," Will coos.

"I don't like Doritos," I sneer.

"Whatever you like, sweetheart, I got you," he reaches out for a hug and I push him away.

He looks at D who just hunches his shoulders at him.

Nicole rolls her eyes, which reads *tell him.*

"Would y'all like some popcorn?" D offers while breaking the tension.

"I told you," I whisper to Nicole. I will admit this is my first, sorta date. Sorta because I am definitely not allowed to date until . . . . The age is still up for debate because my mom is good with 16 and my dad is good with never. I have watched enough TV shows like *The Cosby Show, A Different World* and *Saved By the Bell* to know how this works. If it wasn't a date, I would have already bought snacks for me and Nicole. Nevertheless, I heard the boy must buy the snacks if he is really feeling you.

"I would love some," Will rubs his stomach. "Brother got the munchies, you know, Monica?"

"Hold up, you don't have any money? I thought you said you got me?" I scoff, beyond irritated.

"I can't even get a hug but you want me to buy you some popcorn?" Will throws his hands up in protest.

"I don't hug strangers," I roll my neck extra hard.

"Ah, Monica, can I see you for a minute?" D pulls me on the other side of the arcade out of earshot and sight of Nicole and Will.

"Please talk to your girl, D. She's seriously trippin'," calls out Will.

"Why are you being so rude?" D demands.

"I don't like him, D," I declare, throwing my hands up, ready for this date to be over but I promised Nicole I would be honest with D.

"You just met him. Give him a chance."

"Just like how you're giving Nicole, *my friend*, a chance?"

While giving me a crazy look, he throws his hands up in the air mimicking, *what gives?*

"Out of all the people you want to double date with, it has to be my friend, my homie. You couldn't like anyone else?" I pop off, seeing the perfect opportunity to confess my feelings to D.

"Hold up! Hold up!" He paces back and forth. I guess he is trying to find the right words to say. Rubbing his temples, he gasps, "I know you ain't getting salty over me thinking Nicole is cute. I don't like her. Will's feeling you or at least he was. It was cool to invite your friend. She has been jocking me in class so—"

"She has been scoping out Will. She told me," I boast, laughing.

"What? When? Why didn't you tell me this, so I don't look stupid?"

"Me and you haven't been talking like that. And I was mad at you."

"Mad at me? For what? You said we can't be together."

Tell him how you feel, Monica.

"Yeah, but—"

Don't forget who your father is, Monica.

D throws his hands out in disgust then peeps around the corner to see Will and Nicole walking into the movie theater hand in hand. First, he looks shocked then this sly grin appears on his face as he moves in closer to me. Is he wearing cologne? He never wears cologne. Perfect, hypnotizing cologne.

Monica, stay strong, you can handle him.

Why is your heart beating so fast?

I immediately look away to gather myself.

"Monica, look at me," he implores.

I take a deep breath then stare into those gorgeous brown eyes.

The smile that stretches across his face makes the butterflies match the pace of my heartbeat. Then he parts those soft lips to ask, "I guess you couldn't forget how you feel about a brotha?"

The moment I asked to redeem my foolish request to forget how we feel is here, yet I wish I could get out of this craziness. I have to answer, yet I'm frozen. I don't know what to say to him. I'm so nervous that I don't know if I can say what I feel. I have heard that actions speak louder than words, and I do miss kissing D. I take a deep breath, bite down on my lip and I look around to make sure no one is looking before I grab D by the shirt and lay one big fat kiss on him.

After finally letting him up for air, D has to get it together before speaking again. "Whoa, ummm, okay. I think I see what you did there, but I'm still confused."

"I want to be with you," I let the words gush out of my mouth like a dam bursting. There is no turning back now.

"What about what you said?"

"Forget what I said."

"What about your dad?"

"I guess we will figure that out later."

"MJ, are you sure about this? I can't be going back and forth with you." He puts some distance between us. He eyes me to ensure I won't break his heart again.

"I'm positive. Scared but I'm sure."

"I don't want you to do something that makes you uncomfortable."
I kiss him again.
It takes him a minute to gather himself again then he finally utters, "So we really doing this?"
"Yes!"
"Alright, bet!" He grabs my hand to go into the movie theater but stops like he forgot something. "You want your popcorn with extra butter and a cherry coke?"
"You know me so well."
"That I do, Monica James A.K.A. my MJ. That I do."
While I shake my head in disbelief that I battled my own nerves, I watch him saunter toward the concession stand. I can't believe I kissed him multiple times. I can't believe I said I don't care what my father thinks about us when I know he can flip this situation around. It isn't that I don't care. I'm just hoping that Mom and I can convince my dad to chill. I'm in junior high so I'm almost a teenager.
Because I don't want to be grossed out by Will and Nicole already being lovey, dovey, kissy, kissy, I pick our seats four rows in front of them. I don't know what she sees in Will, but she feels the same way about me and D. She thinks Will is cuter than D. D is too high yella for her while Will is the perfect shade of chocolate.
D brings my snacks after I see him slip Will some cash. He is so triflin'. How you gonna come to the movies with no money? You invite us to the movies, and you have no money. I can't deal.
After the movie, we say our goodbyes inside because we have to act like we didn't plan a date. Our parents will never trust us if they found out. Will and D convinced their parents to let them stay for a second movie and Will is spending the night.
"So let's get this straight." D pulls me in close. "You my girl now?"
I hesitate to answer because I'm still worried about my dad.
"What about..." I'm literally thinking of a master plan.
"Monica, you can't play me like this," he insists.
"Yes, Monica, please give the boy a chance," Nicole intervenes.
"Listen to your homegirl," Will pleads.
"I think we got it," I scoff at Will.
"I don't know why you are still trippin'. You got your boy. Everyone is with who they really want to be with," Will reminds me

"What? You was all up—" I start to argue.

"Stay over there, Will," D asserts then lowers his voice, "Monica, you can't do this and walk away. Obviously, you can't ignore what you feel so let's stop playing and do this." He kisses me on the forehead.

His kiss gives me the confidence to finally tell my dad about D and I. *It will be okay,* I try to convince myself.

As Nicole and I walk outside without the boys, my mom is waiting, and I notice my dad is in the car, too.

"What is your dad doing in the car?" Nicole asks nervously. My mom dropped us off earlier

"I don't know but this doesn't look good." I notice the look on his face that has us both nervous.

The fact that my mom is driving and not him could be a good sign. He has to be in a relaxed mood not to drive.

"How was the movie, girls?" my dad questions. He doesn't look relaxed at all.

"It was pretty good," Nicole answers happily.

"Daddy, I'm surprised not to see you driving," I attempt to lighten the mood.

"My car broke down, so your mom picked me up."

"Where is TJ?" I know they wouldn't let him stay home by himself.

"You know he is hanging out with Nick today," Dad points out.

"I forgot." I look at Nicole, who immediately looks out the window. She knows Nick is D's brother.

"You know what else you forgot?" Dad turns around to face me, "To tell us you were meeting D and what's that other boy's name?" He faces my mom briefly.

"I don't remember the child's name. He's new to their neighborhood," Mom comments.

"What's his name, Monica?" my dad demands trying to keep his cool while eyeing me.

"His name is Will, Dad," I shudder.

"Yeah, Will … so pretty much you going on dates now?" He doesn't break eye contact.

"No, Daddy, we were just hanging out," I appeal.

"Monica, you act like I was born yesterday. If y'all were just hanging out, you would have told your mother them boys were going to be there.

We take y'all out all the time. Why the secrets?" He throws his hands up as he turns back around.

"Daddy, you know if I would have asked then Nick and TJ would have to come, too. They get on my nerves."

"TJ is your brother. He is supposed to get on your nerves," Dad retorts.

I look out the window and notice the Jennings's passing by us in their car without Daliyah. Immediately, I jerk around to see her and another girl sauntering into the movies. Nicole sees what I see but tries to hide her disgust along with me.

"Hello, earth to Monica? I know you hear me. Was this a date?" Daddy snatches me back to attention.

"Dad, we were just hanging out. You said I can't date until I'm thirty-five," I retort.

"If we weren't in front of company… Be mindful of your words, Monica," my mom reprimands.

"And that attitude!" my dad bellows while facing me.

"You not going to lie and have a disrespectful attitude. Don't do that, Monica, especially when you know we could, " my mom stops to take a deep breath. "Don't get embarrassed in front of your friend." My mom is fuming while eyeballing me through the rearview mirror.

"We can't trust you if you're going to lie!" my dad barks.

"Manipulate the system," my mother interjects. "If you want to hang out with D, your brothers have to come."

"End of story! You don't just up and change the rules when you feel like it," Dad reiterates sternly then throws his hands up again. "All this lying got me wondering. Something happened with you and D before?"

"Daddy, do we have to have this conversation in front of Nicole?" I beg my dad to let us discuss this another time.

"You doggone skippy! Because the next time you attempt to plan some foolishness like this, she will remind you your pops and moms will cut your life short."

Fighting back tears, I can't believe they are doing this, especially right now.

"Nicole, you know I have to speak to your mom about what happened today," my mom assures.

"Yes, ma'am," Nicole acknowledges.

"Monica, we gonna have to sit down and talk with the Browns. This can't happen again," my daddy orders. "Ain't going to have no twelve-year-olds unsupervised in a dark movie theater. You must have lost your mind, Monica. I'm not going to even ask what I think happened besides you watching a movie with a boy. Not just a girl but a boy. And you had a boy, too, Nicole?" He looks back at her in disbelief then faces the front of the car.

"I can't handle all this growing up. What happened to Barbies and Cabbage Patch Kids? Why you gotta be liking boys? Wasn't trying to use the shotgun until you were sixteen."

"Daddy, don't do this!" I cry.

"What are you crying for? You acting like someone is physically hurting you and D. Just gotta lay out the law. My name is Lawrence!"

"Lawrence, you know the girl likes the boy," my mom snitches.

"Likes who? Not D! She better not be liking the boy we allow in her room!"

I can tell Nicole is trying not to laugh at my crazy family.

"Oh, I forgot I didn't tell you," my mom admits biting her lip.

"Thanks a lot, Mom. Glad I can tell you anything," I groan.

"I just assumed your daddy knew. It is so obvious. LB you didn't know? Please tell me you knew."

"Of course, I didn't know! He was up in her room! I ain't playing with Monica about having any boyfriends, Cynthia! Matter of fact, she could always have boyfriends but their names are Math, Social Studies, Science, ELA... they don't mind if you cheat on them."

As mad as I am, I want to laugh at what my dad just said. I understand being focused on my studies, but they will not be the object of my affection. I don't know why he is acting like I wasn't going to grow up one day. Again, I'm practically a teenager... almost a woman.   It's not like I'm with a guy who gets in trouble in school, has bad grades and is disrespectful. I don't talk to ruffnecks.

D is a very good dude, a rare type of brother to encounter. He isn't trying to be thug nation like some of these other wannabes. He doesn't chase girls like Lou. Honestly, he doesn't have to try because girls come on to him and are willing to do whatever he commands, which adds another plus that he doesn't go for the fast girls. It says a lot about a young man who could get any girl he wanted, but he is selective because he knows she is a reflection of his character. He is a gentleman who opens doors. Whoever heard of a seventh grade boy opening your door unless he wanted something from you? All around, he is a genuine, good, fun guy.

I need my daddy to get it together. This is humiliating torture. I didn't mean to disappoint my mom because, again, I can come to her about anything. Nevertheless, she doesn't believe in hiding anything from my dad and I know they would send the rugrats if I told her Nicole and I were meeting up with Will and D. I couldn't risk ruining my plans.

Honestly, I didn't have a plan. Nicole told me I should be honest with D but I had no clue what that would look like. I didn't think it would go down so early between us at the movie theater, but Will set me off when he didn't have any money and he had the nerve to invade my space *again*.

How does Nicole see anything likable about him?

Unlike me, Nicole told her mom we were meeting boys at the movies. She said her mom trusts her, so she knows she wasn't going to do anything crazy. Sometimes I wonder how much my mom trusts me because they always send the rugrats behind us unless they choose to go somewhere else. I just want to be alone with my boyfriend. Even if we weren't boyfriend and girlfriend, it is cool to hang out without the rugrats. Now how we hang will be totally different, and I won't see the inside of any movie theater for a very long time unless I'm accompanied by adults.

I hope my dad won't ring his neck and will at least let him stay my boyfriend. Some would say cows with pigs as their copilots would have to jump over the moon before that happens.

CHAPTER 9

I'M A G

Nicole "Nikki" Myers

Monica's family has to be the funniest ever. It takes everything in me not to laugh at her crying at her dad trippin'. I'm used to girls crying because they found out they were pregnant and they had to tell their fathers, not because they have a boyfriend or had to lie about a date. I need them both to swallow the biggest chill pill possible.

I was upfront with my mom because she knows I ain't trying to be fresh. More than anything, she trusts me and knows I won't do anything that compromises this precious, beautiful temple her and my dad taught me to treasure.

I witnessed too many cousins not that much older than me give up their childhood because they let some dude make them look stupid. Some of the dudes are triflin' bums. These girls are so focused on love and landing a man, who is really a boy, that they forget about the parenting part. *How foolish.* Stupid… I can't and I won't be the one.

"Your mom and dad aren't home?" Mrs. James worries when she notices there are no cars in the driveway.

Yes!

"They must have stepped out for a bit," I assume. My older sister is on the front porch doing what she does best, yap her trap on the phone. I'm surprised she is not at the mall or the skating rink. She waves at Mrs. James, letting her know she sees us.

"I will call her later," Mrs. James advises. I'm cool with later because it gives me time to tell Mom the story. Hopefully, she will act surprised when Mrs. James calls. I know Monica will get into more trouble if her mom finds out I told my mom, and she didn't tell hers. I moved to this side of town to get away from drama and stepped right into some.

"Thank you so much for the ride. Monica, I guess I will see you later. Nice meeting you, Mr. James."

Monica and her father both mumble their goodbyes while Mrs. James is Mrs. Sunshine. She waits for me to get on the front porch before backing out of our long driveway that has perfectly manicured bushes outlining it. Before pulling off, she honks the horn.

"What is up with your girl? She looks depressed," inquires Rayshon. My parents really love their names because my sister and I both have some part of their names in ours. My dad's name is Raymond and my mom's name is Nicolette. My sister is Rayshon Nicolette and I'm Nicole Raymona. Some people call it ghetto while I call it pride in who they are.

I sit in the rocking chair next to her, chuckling, "You are so doggone nosy. You got off the phone to hear the 411?"

"Spill it, girl!" Rayshon prompts.

"Monica didn't tell her folks we were meeting boys today." I laugh.

"How did they find out?" She perks up in her chair.

"Her younger brother is over at Donovan's house now, so I'm pretty sure it came up in conversation."

"What is the deal between those two?"

I give Rayshon the whole spill, including what happened earlier at the movies.

"You know some daddies want their girls to stay little forever. Our pops seems chill about a lot of stuff. He trusts us."

"True that!"

We both start rocking in our chairs in unison, which has become one of our past times.

One of the reasons my mom moved us to the suburbs, or what my homies call the White side of town, was to get away from the hood. She was tired of having teacher conferences and dealing with suspensions over my temper.

I hung with the baddest chicks, including my cousin, Slice, so it made sense for me to join her crew. Slice was never down with me pledging and she knew my parents would kill me once I made my vow. She got her nickname from her fighting style.

Last year I snatched the title of being the baddest chick at Shaw by beating down several girls, including Antonia Mickle, a former bully. Her reputation as a fireball whose flames engulfed people put fear in the hearts of many, including teachers. When that happened, the crew went behind Slice's back to try and recruit me.

She was heated and wasn't trying to watch her favorite baby cousin jack up her life, so she had a talk with me.

"You can't be like me. I love you, so let me handle the lightweights. If they step to you, I got something for them. Go to school and handle your business. Keep 'dem grades up and ya' nose clean. There's no life in what I do. I'm surprised I'm still alive. You and Rayshon can be the first grands to get outta here, go to college and make Granny proud. Trust me when I say you don't want this life. You got too much to live for, ya' hear?"

As much as I didn't want to listen, I knew she was right.

Fifth grade was a rough year because my dad was away fighting in the Gulf War and then sixth grade they reassigned him out of state for a whole freaking year. I was pissed, so I channeled my anger into the hype of being this bad girl. I was attending the school marked as the land where Slice once reigned with terror. Foolishly, I wanted to keep the tradition going.

Despite constantly getting suspended, I never had lower than an A in any of my classes. It bothered the mess out of teachers that I was so smart because some would rather I be a dumb trouble-maker. I would never talk about my grades and acted like I didn't care about work. Teachers also refused to recognize how smart I am. I would never participate, just sit in the back of the room and be quiet. Honestly, I think that is what they wanted. Just another Black face they felt wouldn't amount to anything.

When I finally told my mom what teachers were telling me, she quickly scheduled a meeting right before my expulsion hearing with the principal, the assistant principal, all my teachers and she even called her friend who works at the district office. I wish you could have seen the look on their faces when Mrs. Dina walked through the door right before the meeting started. I wasn't ratting them out hoping I wouldn't get expelled. I was ready to be done with them and that stupid school. Nevertheless, I got tired of telling my mom nothing was wrong and I didn't care. I told her everything.

Mrs. Dina Hawkins is technically my principal, Mr. Kingston's, boss so the nervous tension on his and my teacher's faces is hilarious to me. Of course, they don't understand why she is here and my mother explained she had more concerns that needed to be addressed before the hearing. Normally, a meeting before the hearing isn't granted. Given the sensitivity of the matter, Mrs. Hawkins had them make an exception.

"Nicole, please tell them what you told me the other day," my mother urges.

Gasping for air because I never spoke up for myself, I hear my father in my ear, "Don't let them punk you. When you get in that meeting, don't let anyone intimidate you out of the truth. You hear me?"

"Nicole—" my mom nudges me, bringing me back to reality.

"Well, umm, last week when I got into another fight, Ms. Wells told me I was nothing. She said I have all those brains and it is a waste. She then said 'I will end up locked up in jail like Slice or dead."

The whole time Mrs. Dina is writing notes then looking up at the teacher.

"I spoke with Ms. Wells. She has apologized," adds Mr. Kingston.

"I would like to hear from Ms. Wells," interrupts Mrs. Dina.

"Ms. Wells?" Mr. Kingston gives her clearance.

She is turning red and I can tell she didn't expect to speak. I know how these teachers operate.

"Well, I was just reprimanding Nicole for being in another fight," Ms. Wells bickers after taking too long to answer the question.

"What exactly did you say, Ms. Wells?" Mrs. Dina asks, peering intensely through her soul.

"What I meant to say is that if she doesn't straighten up her act and get it together like the intelligent young lady she is, she will end up in prison," Ms. Well stammers.

"Ms. Wells, I want you to realize you are talking to a professional who is very capable of reading in between the lines," Mrs. Dina emphasizes. "What you meant to say and exactly what you said are two different stories. What exactly did you say to Miss Myers?"

Fumbling for words to say, I can tell she is letting her anger get the best of her. "Why am I being persecuted? Nicole is the problem here. She can't properly resolve her anger, and I'm on trial?"

"Ms. Wells, I'm going to be clear with you. We are not excusing the actions of Miss Myers," Mrs. Dina clarifies. "Nevertheless, we can't resolve the complaint of a parent if you won't own up to what was done. You have yet to tell us what was said and refusing to doesn't lessen the consequences."

"The consequences of what?" Ms. Wells retorts.

"Your actions."

"What did I do?"

"What did you say, Ms. Wells?" Mrs. Dina gives her one more chance to admit what she did was wrong. Ms. Wells takes too long to answer and Mrs. Dina sighs out of frustration.

"Let's move on. I didn't make time in my schedule to deal with a serious issue in a juvenile way." Mrs. Dina flips over her notes then looks at all the teachers. "Last I checked, we are professionals, teachers who are inspiring hope into the future of this world through our students."

"Mrs. Hawkins, may I interject?" pleads Mr. Pope.

"You may," she beckons.

"I think sometimes you all forget what it is like to be in the classroom with students like Nicole."

"See what you are not going to do is ostracize my daughter," my mother interjects.

"Students like me, Mr. Pope? What do you mean by that?" I pause and wait for a response, which never comes. "I have maintained all A's since I began attending this school. Yes, I get into fights but has anyone stopped to ask why? No, I just get suspended. Y'all tell my mom I'm home for a few days and that's it. You don't care. How are you a teacher and don't care?"

I look around the room and none of the teachers are making eye contact with me because they know I'm telling the truth.

"Mr. Kingston and your faculty, Mrs. Myers asked me to attend your conference today because she is disturbed by the culture. I'm disturbed by the culture. These kids always feel like failures. Imagine how Nicole could be different if someone took the time to invest in her. Did you ever think about that, Mr. Kingston?"

"If you took the time to care, you would know or remember because I'm pretty sure I told you about our situation," Mom assures them. "Maybe you just didn't believe a family living in the hood could have a father in the *home, but we do. He has been deployed on different assignments for two years. Between both of our daughters, Rayshon, who y'all never had a problem with, and Nicole, Nicole is the closest to her father. You never wondered how someone from the same supportive family is acting opposite of our values. But you don't see her as Nicole, you see her as another Black face who you can't wait to push on unprepared. It baffles you my daughter fights but stays on the A-honor-roll."*

"Mrs. H-Hawkins," Mr. Kingston stammers while ignoring what my mother just said, "We have looked into intervention methods."

"Again, y'all think you are dealing with a stupid woman," Mrs. Dina interrupts. "First, you didn't acknowledge what Mrs. Myers just said or apologized. Looked into and implementing them are two different actions. All you did was perpetuate the school-to-prison pipeline. I'm done. Please know this matter isn't resolved.   We are not going to come to a resolution today. Mrs. Myers and Miss Myers, I apologize we couldn't come to a reasonable solution. Nevertheless, please know a feasible solution will be implemented and not looked into. Mr. Kingston, we will be in touch. Have a good day."

As we exit the conference room, Mr. Kingston is the only one who walks us out while the teachers are boiling over with anger. I don't know if I feel relief because I was finally able to let out what I have been holding onto for so long or scared for my life knowing I had to come back to school and face these jokers.

I couldn't fathom spending my last month of school at Shaw. As a result, the board agreed to let me be homeschooled by my mother. Soon after, my parents decided we were moving. The move would put me at Alice Drive Jr. High.

Although my mom had me attending counseling ever since she saw the angry streak in me rise to the surface, she now understood part of that anger to fight was fueled by being in an environment where I felt unwanted.

But let's be real.

I didn't fight just to fight.

I just won't let anyone come at me crazy. Talking smack to me or my crew will get you punched in the face. It is simple and plain. My sister is the same way, but she doesn't get into as many fights as me because she is really afraid of my mom and dad. If she is pushed in a corner, feeling a need to literally defend herself, she feels justified in knocking someone out.

Once Daddy got home, he retired from the military but still wanted to work to keep busy. He doesn't have to work but he can't sit around the house with my mom all day. I'll admit I can't either. She gets aggravating because she can't just chill sometimes. She always has to be busy.

Now I'm over here in freaking Mayberry. At first, I did wonder how they could stand all this quiet. There is nothing like block parties ending up broken up by gunfire because some dude is mad at another dude who made a move on his girl. We didn't need to watch soap operas because we could hear our neighbors. There was always something happening.

"What are you going to tell Momma?" Shon interrupts my thoughts.

"There is nothing to tell her. She already knew but I do want her to act surprised for Monica's sake. Monica and her mom are pretty close."

"Apparently, not that close."

I had to assure Shon Monica and her mom are super close because she told her about the kiss with Donovan, which causes me to blurt out, "I kissed him!"

I'm blushing so hard. I didn't even know that was possible with my chocolate skin.

"Hold up? What?" she screams.

"It was a little sloppy, but it was so dreamy." I look into the clouds imagining the kiss again. Shon snaps me back to reality.

"Why is your nose so wide open?"

I literally touch my nose then swing at her intending to miss. My sister packs a mean punch. Then I have to remind her, "I told you I'm feeling him."

"Your first crush," she coos.

"Yeah, my first crush."

My first kiss, too. What is really going on with me? No boy has ever had me open like this. I give Shon the whole run down of the date switcharoo and why I'm so into Will.

"He is so freaking cute and so freaking arrogant, but it is sexy!"

"Please don't use that word around Mom. She will trip."

"I'm not talking to Mom. I'm talking to you. I can't quite explain it. He is just fine and it is not just his looks. Like, I know he went after Monica but the way he did it was hot! He knows what he wants, and he goes after it."

"You just met him so keep your eyes open." She gets up to stretch before heading into the house. I follow her, and she opens the storm door to let me walk in first.

"Don't even try to play me, Shon. You know how I do. I got this."

"Your nose is wide open, lil' sis', so you better watch yourself."

POETIC INTERMISSION

Nicole Myers

Do You Really See Me?

Amid your frustration, rage, negative criticism,
do you notice I'm unfazed?
Desensitized, no longer pushing toward the prize.
Blocking out and hurdling any comments
intentionally not boosting my esteem.
Knowing you meant to tear me down
only pushes me further in the darkness.
I'm quick to thrash any chick who crosses the line.
Academics, I speak fluently, excellently.
Babble is what you mumble while trying to fathom how.
Do you not see the wall I have built?
I don't, I can't hear you.
   Unlike the battle of Jericho,
my wall won't come tumbling down with your loud shouts.
Desperately crave sincerity.
Missing my daddy has me angry.
Yet, you never ask, question, or inquire.
Just waiting for me to expire rather than dig deeper into my soul.
Find out why it is so cold.
Desperate for someone to care
Maybe this frozen shell will melt.

CHAPTER 10

LOVE IS FOR SUCKAS

William "Will" Johnson

Earlier at the Movies

"Did I just watch you dive across this movie theater like you're GI Joe on a secret mission?" I mock.

"Monica's dad, Mr. James, W-Wild Lawrence—" D stammers while trying to stay out of sight.

"Isn't that your godfather? Why are you trippin'?" I challenge.

"Yo, if you knew her father, you wouldn't say I'm trippin'."

D drops some knowledge by admitting Monica's dad doesn't believe his daughter should have a boyfriend until she is fifty. He's overprotective of his babygirl. I get it, but D is a good dude, his godson.

I pat him on the back. "I'll say your eulogy at your funeral."

"Shut up! Mr. James isn't that wild."

"If you saw the way you tucked and rolled—" I buckle over in laughter, "I'm surprised you don't have carpet burn. Based on your wanna be double-oh-seven skills, looks like you were in fear for your life, son."

If he wasn't so nervous, I think he would have laughed at my humor. I don't understand going through all this drama for one girl. There are so many girls out there. I found that out this weekend when my date switched from Monica to Nicole. He claims he believes Monica is the girl for him, just like his dad knew his mom was the woman for him at a young age.

Speaking of other girls being out there, Daliyah Jennings, Monica's sworn enemy, comes strolling through the door with her eyes set on her prize: Donovan.

"What is she doing here?" he doesn't even attempt to keep his voice down, and she doesn't seem to be the one to back down from any challenge.

"I thought you would be happy to see me. Where did your date go?"

"My girlfriend had to go home," he grits.

"Girlfriend? Who, Monifah?"

"Yo, I know we agreed to watch another movie but we can dip. Shorty obviously wants to cause drama," I intervene.

"This *shorty* has a first name," Daliyah retorts.

Ironically, D decides he wants to stay to watch the second movie. I think he's more terrified of going home and facing the consequences of his parents finding out about our date with the girls than possibly being spotted with Daliyah.

Before I pull D into the movie theater, I face Daliyah, "Don't start nothin', won't be nothin' so leave us alone. Don't come sit near us. D told you Monica is his girl so back off."

Surprisingly, she listens but she looks like she is up to something. She keeps staring D down but he isn't paying her any attention. He is buggin' the whole time, wondering how his parents are going to trip and agonizing over how Monica's dad is going to react to all this. I told him to stop trippin' because her dad probably didn't see him. For all we know, the parents don't know about our date.

When the movie is over we go outside and spot his mom. At first I thought my assumptions were right because his mom doesn't look a bit upset. When she passes by TBCY, The County's Best Yogurt, which is supposed to be our first stop before kickin' it tonight, I started to have doubts. Who doesn't want frozen yogurt before piggin' out on pizza?

D is in such a daze he doesn't notice we are passing it, and I don't think I should bring it up. Maybe she forgot about it.

With her poker face, she utters these words in the most chill tone ever, "Will, I know you are supposed to spend the night tonight, but we had a family matter come up. We are going to have to do it another time."

Before getting out of the car, I turn to Donovan and wish him good luck then thank her for the ride. I don't even attempt to dap up my boy who still looks shook. Now I see why he wanted to put this off as long as possible.

As I walk into my house with my bookbag, my mom gives me a strange look because she expected me to spend the night with my new homie. Somehow my mom will find out why Donovan is in trouble so I might as well brace for the blast of her wrath now. I'm used to my mom blowing up over everything, and I will make it worse by acting like nothing happened.

"Plans changed. Donovan got into trouble because we met girls at the movie theater." I hunch my shoulders and walk to the kitchen.

She follows me. "William Michael Johnson, I know you—"

"No big deal! I promise you!" I cut her off. I look in the fridge for something to drink hoping the cool air would cool her off.

"You are not allowed to date. Why would y'all think it is okay to meet girls there?" She slams the fridge door, luckily it was after I grab a can of soda. I take a seat at the table where it will be easier to withstand her anger. She turns to look at my dad who is walking in to hopefully save me. "You knew about this the whole time?"

Here we go.

"Knew about what?" my dad asked, opening up the fridge to also get something to drink. "What are you doing home, Will?"

"You better talk to your son, Mike. I will not be anyone's grandma!" my mom adds, snapping her neck and widening her eyes in my father's direction. Despite knowing my mom can be very dramatic, I'd rather deal with it now and give her time to cool off. I would love to talk on the phone with Nicole. Based on her reaction, I hope she doesn't yank any opportunity to make that call.

"Why you always gotta say that, Mom? No one is having sex. I'm fine but not that fine," I mock the way she was speaking because I'm so aggravated and immediately regret my tone when my dad speaks up next.

"Will don't get punched in the chest," my dad lowers his voice while joining me at the table. I don't even open my mouth. I know exactly what that tone means. My dad doesn't play about disrespect when it comes to my mom or any adult.

Let's be real. I don't believe in disrespecting my mom either. I love her, but her level of drama could easily cast her on any soap opera. I sometimes allow my aggravation to get the best of me. I know where babies come from and I ain't doing any of that with girls. I wish she would get that.

After he stares me down to make sure I understand, he looks at my mom and says, "Sharon, what are you talking about?"

"Tell him." She pulls out a chair for herself. Before I can comply, my brothers run in the room.

"What are we telling?" Robert, my youngest, nosey little brother, asks.

"Y'all are so nosy," I complain. "Go play." The last thing I want to do is let them hear that I went on a double date. They'd never let me live that down.

"I'm hungry." Harrison says as he heads to the fridge. Thankfully, he doesn't seem to care about the conversation they interrupted.

"Me too," Rob echoes, forgetting about his former question.

"Why don't I fix you all something to eat? Y'all can eat in the family room," my mom beams, then goes to fix them snacks. For once in my life, I'm thankful for the interruption. My mom went from nearly knocking my head off back to happy just that quickly.

"We can eat in the family room!" Rob shouts. "Will, what did you do?" I cringe at that last question. Just when I thought I was home free, he brought up the elephant in the room.

"Can we eat on my favorite tray?" As usual, Harrison doesn't pay Rob any attention.

"Go in the room and Mom will bring you something to eat. Go," our dad demands, tired of the sidebar and ready to get back to business.

They both scurry their way out of the kitchen without another word, leaving me to my fate.

"Now what happened?" Dad leans back in his chair.

"Donovan and I met some girls at the movies."

Dad goes to smile but my mom snatches it off his face with her eyes.

"That's not good," Dad attempts to keep it serious.

"No, it's not good," she is whispering but it feels like she is yelling at me. She gets up to fix the boys' food. "We don't need our almost teenage boy alone in the dark with girls. You know what happens in the dark, Mike!" She snatches the fridge door open. I'm surprised she didn't take it off the hinges.

"Not all kids do those things in the dark, Sharon. Calm down, " my dad assures.

"I'm calm!" She slams the fridge door and then takes a deep breath before speaking again, "I'm calm."

"I'm not stupid. Y'all had the talk with me. I understand what not to do. Why are you tripp—" my mom glares at me, "Why are you so upset, Ma?" I grumble.

"Technically, you lied, son," Dad reminds me. "You made it seem like you and your boy were hanging out at the movies. We didn't know about the girls. You know how that looks?" In the midst of my mom's grunts of agreement, she is slamming drawers and cabinet doors along with the mayonnaise jar. Let me make that amount of ruckus when I'm mad. I wouldn't live to tell it.

"Yeah, Dad," I sigh. "But nothing happened. Yeah, I kissed the girl but that was it."

Why did I let that come out of my mouth? Stupid.

"I can't." My mom takes the food to my brothers while shaking her head like I got someone pregnant.

"Dad, talk to her!" I throw my hands up pleading for my life.

"Talk her out of killing you or trusting you to leave this house again?" He goes to pour himself a glass of water.

"Can I at least talk on the phone?" I whisper. "The girl I kissed… I want to call her later."

"You really like this girl," he lowers his voice then leans back into his chair.

"Yo, Dad, she is mad cool and so fly. I can't *not* call her after us having a dope time. She'll think I'm ignoring her."

"I may be able to work that out. Just be real with us. Don't do this again. You can't have your mom mad at me, too."

"She shouldn't be mad at me, either. I didn't do anything." My dad widens his eyes, as he often does when I'm not listening. "Okay, okay! I didn't do the thing but I did a thing because I didn't tell y'all everything." He nods his head in approval. "But, Dad, I need y'all to know I ain't out here doing it. Not saying I don't think about sex, but I pay attention to the sex ed videos. I ain't trying to have my junk look like those photos."

"Smart man. Next time you plan a date, let us know so we can supervise. Maybe even get one of your cousins to watch y'all."

I hear my mom fussing at my brothers who are arguing over who received more food.

"Go to your room. I'll talk to your mom." We give each other a pound.

"Thanks, Dad."

Despite being told I'm on punishment, no phone or video games, and I can't go outside for at least a week, my dad is looking out for his boy. He tells Mom they have to run errands and the little bros actually want to tag along. I have the house to myself and time to sneak a phone call.

"I told Donovan I thought you had the hots for me," I laugh.

"I think we both know we had the hots for each other. I saw you peeping me out in class, Will," Nicole retorts.

"You got me! Ain't gonna lie. Was Monica acting all stank part of the plan?"

According to Nicole, there was no plan. At the end of the day, both of us believe Monica and Donovan should have been upfront with everyone, including each other, from the beginning. Why would he let me holla at someone he claims to be in love with? I'm still trippin' on how I totally missed he is feeling her. Nicole tells me boys don't get it.

"I know you ain't dissin' a brother, an honor roll student athlete."

"Perception, common sense and intelligence are not one and the same. Know that, homie. I saw it written all over her face."

"She didn't have to say a word, huh?"

"What you know about The Rude Boys?"

"Your dog loves R&B. Play your cards right and I may even sing for you."

"Go 'head."

"Naw, can't have you sweatin' me! You think I'm fine now? What do you think will happen when I serenade you?" I prop my feet up on the kitchen table.

Monica detested my cockiness. I call it confidence. Nicole loves it. I'm really diggin' this girl because she gets me and knows what she wants. D and Monica should learn from us.

"Speaking of your boy, you heard from him?"

"How am I supposed to? I'm not supposed to be talking to you, remember?"

"You snuck to call me. I'm pretty sure you called to check on your boy."

"You're right."

"Can't play me, son." She giggles.

"His dad let me talk to him for a bit. He is supposed to be meeting with Monica's dad. That wouldn't be me."

"Love will do that to you sometimes."

"What is up with everyone and this *l-word?* I don't see how or why D, Monica or anyone thinks they love someone. We are too young for that."

"I know. It is not like I don't believe in love but I don't believe in finding *the one* this early in life. If it doesn't work out, it doesn't work out. Move on."

We both believe that fact, which is why this match is perfect. After finding out she likes R&B, I had to find out if she loves rap, which she does. We both share the same favorite rapper, Tupac.

"Can I be honest with you about something?"

"Of course."

She's hesitating. "I don't usually... That was my first kiss.. I mean, technically, I just met you and—"

"I have that effect on girls," I tease.

"Now who sounds like a playa?"

I had to let Nicole know there is no player in me when she started trying to convince me she isn't easy. I had to assure her I never believed she was easy. I would call it assertive. She knew what she wanted and went for it. Kissing also meant she is really feeling a brotha.

We agreed that I'm not her boyfriend, but I can carry her books to class. *I can dig that.*

CHAPTER 11

MAN TO MAN

Donovan Brown

I underestimated the trouble meeting MJ at the movies alone would cause. I knew it would be an issue and it didn't help that I didn't tell my parents, either. Yet, I need our parents to understand they don't have to worry. Thankfully, my moms and pops didn't chew me out like I know Monica's parents did to her.

"I hope today was the best day of your life!" my mom hisses.

"Not sure if I'm supposed to answer that question," I mumble.

"Your smart butt knows that wasn't even a question. Statement of fact! If it was a question, you know it was rhetorical!" Her eyes shoot lasers through the rearview mirror.

"I wasn't trying to be disrespectful, Ma. I apologize if it came out that way," I throw my hands up in protest.

"How do you think this whole situation looks? You know how I feel about lying, Donovan, so don't do this again." My mom takes a deep breath and lowers her tone. "Your dad and I both know you're coming of age, but we don't believe in twelve-year-old boys and girls being unsupervised."

"Yes, ma'am." I look at her through her rearview mirror. My dad is in the house with the boys. Will sleeping over was canceled because of the lie. She reminds me it is important to always tell the truth, and omitting details is a form of lying. She reiterates they, my parents taught me better than that. Then she drops the bomb on me by alerting me that everyone already knew I liked MJ and that we kissed.

I just look at her. I'm not freaking out because I know my dad is down to earth. I just want to know if *everyone* includes Mr. James. *I'm too young to die.*

I sit back in the seat and just close my eyes, wishing we could start this day, this week, this whole summer all over again. Now I see why Monica was so hesitant about us being together. We both got caught up in the moment, in the kiss. Our hearts want what they want despite the consequences.

MJ could have just said I gave her the bracelet like I told my dad. She didn't have to mention the kiss. I told my dad about giving the girl I like the bracelet. I wonder if he knew this whole time the girl was MJ? But now that they know I have to pray Mrs. Cynthia can come through for us. Mrs. Cynthia is known to win anyone's heart over so I hope she can convince Mr. James MJ is in good hands with me.

"You think Mrs. Cynthia told Mr. James?" I speculate

"I don't know. I just really hope he won't blow this out of proportion. He is going to trip. At the end of the day, we are like family. We were all once teenagers, so we get it. Hopefully, you can have supervised dates when Lawrence is ready. Just know it will be a minute. Lying about today didn't help matters."

I see my dad working in the garage. He doesn't seem to notice us getting out of the car. I attempt to sneak into the front door.

"D, hand me the wrench, son," he summons me into the garage. *Dang!*

My mom mouths, "It will be okay."

I nod but just want to pop a video game in and chill out. Monica is willing to be my girl and I just feel like her pops will snatch her away from me. I probably can't even call her because he put her on lockdown. I can feel it.

As I get the wrench, I wonder if I should go in the house and change.

"You won't get dirty. Just pass me the tools," he reads my mind. My dad is relentless about wiping down all his tools after he is done using them. "I know you don't want to mess up your gear." He looks up from the car. "You have on cologne, son?"

"Yes sir." I smile then quickly stop when I notice he isn't smiling back. Then, out of the blue, he starts laughing.

"What were you thinking, son?" he jests while wiping his hand on a towel.

"What do you mean?" I'm a little confused. Why is he laughing at my pain?

"You know exactly what I mean. You went on a date with Lawrence James's babygirl, the reason he is a registered gun owner," he chuckles. "And both of you lied about it."

"Well, I didn't ask her to lie, and she technically wasn't coming to see me," I hang my head low, somewhat embarrassed how the date started and how my life may end.

"What?" Now he is the one perplexed.

"See what had happened was... It's a funny story, Dad. Not really, just stupid. Yeah, Monica told me a few weeks ago... after the second kiss—" I start, thinking I might as well tell him everything.

"After the what?" he cackles loudly into tears.

"We kissed... twice."

"When did this happen? Where did it happen?" one of his infamous eyebrows shoots up.

"The last time they came over. We were in the game room. That was the second time."

"When was the first time?" He is leaning back on the truck.

"After I bought her the bracelet. Remember I asked you about a girl I kept dreaming about?"

"That girl was Monica? Wow, son. I had a feeling. Your mom definitely had a feeling. We can't leave y'all alone anymore, eh?"

"All we do... all we *did* was kiss," I plead leaning back on the wall of the garage.

"I believe you son, but what you don't know is kissing leads to other things."

"Like what?"

"I know you know. Don't make us have the talk."

"I mean, I know about *that*, Dad. I'm just not thinking about that."

"Now you're not thinking about that. Things change. People change. You're not a little boy anymore."

Since I'm not a little boy anymore, I tell my dad he should understand why I don't always want to hang out with my brothers. It would be cool if my parents would allow maybe an older cousin to drive us to the movies but it is always Frick and Frack, the most annoying people in the world.

"I get it, son, but you have to understand where Lawrence is coming from. And you forget we were once teenagers, so we have seen some things. We're just trying to keep y'all out of," he hesitates then says, "situations."

"What kind of situations?"

"We're going to have that talk."

"Now?"

I hope not.

He decides we won't have the talk but he definitely wanted to know what type of kiss Monica and I had. I surprised him by stating it was a deep kiss, no tongue. That's enough for me.

"You are more innocent than LB thinks," he shifts his stance.. "We're still having that talk, though."

"Ooookay, back to the story. I asked her out and she said no. I know because of her pops."

"I know… I know. LB and I went to college together and he told me some stories. That's why he is paranoid. He thinks all boys are like him or how he was. Cindy had him on lock. Other women would try to get some LB but he was determined to make Cindy Mrs. James."

"This sucks, Dad! This sucksssssssss!" I began pacing back and forth in the garage to calm myself. My father lets me have my space to breathe so he goes back under the hood of my grandfather's 1970 blue Ford F-150. Out of frustration, I plead, "I know you said I'm too young for love, but I love this girl and Mr. James will snatch her away from me."

"He doesn't see himself snatching anything when she belongs to him. That's his heart. Take into account that you both lied, son. You jacked it up by lying. Lying makes you look suspicious to LB. I don't mind y'all going steady, but no dates or hanging out without telling us. An adult has to be there. If you would have played it right, we all would have been cool with… what's that other girls' name who was there?"

"Nicole… That was my original date." I have to explain to him how I was stupid enough to introduce Will to MJ. Lou was right about MJ never changing how she felt. Dad assures me I have a lot to learn about girls, which is almost a sucker punch. Lou having more common sense than me in this situation is crazy.

"You actually think Mr. James will allow us to date?"

"Eventually, yeah. Lawrence can't keep Monica under lock and key forever. He knows that, but you definitely delayed the possibility."

"I wish I knew how to fix this!"

"Son, you are not in control. You were never in control. You are a young man who is a minor and under the care of adults. You can fix this by abiding by our rules, even when they don't make sense. Since y'all didn't do that, you just gotta let the dust settle and clear. Give Lawrence some time to wrap his head around this. You know it is going to be different when y'all hang out now, right?"

"Yeah, I guess." I hang my head further in disappointment. "Can I go in the house now?"

"I should make you help me. Because of you, nobody got frozen yogurt today, but yeah, I'm done." He watches me walk into the house then goes back to his second wife, the truck.

"Don, are you hungry?" my mom asks standing at the kitchen table ready to give me anything to attempt to lighten the mood.

"Maybe later. I'll be in the playroom." I start heading that way.

"Lou said he might come by after his game tonight," my mom calls after me.

"I thought I couldn't have anyone over." I come back into the kitchen confused.

"You look like you need someone to talk to." The fact that she is backpedaling punishment is crazy and sad. She must know Mr. James is not going to let up.

"Thanks but tell him I don't feel like hanging tonight."

"Son, you have to talk." My mom is trying to make me feel better.

"Me and Dad talked. I'm talked out. I gotta go."

I feel my heart breaking in my chest. I just want to talk to Monica. Hearing her voice right now would calm my nerves. I know I will have to meet with Mr. James but I don't know how I'm going to convince him I'm not that guy. He knows I'm a respectable young man, and I will treat his daughter like the beautiful princess she is.

I find out the next morning I will get the opportunity to prove that point to Mr. James sooner than I thought. I want it but I don't want it. *Why, Lord, why?* During church service, I went to the altar to have one of the ministers pray with me. I didn't tell him why. I just needed help. I keep fumbling in my mind on what to say. My parents tell me I just need to be honest, apologize, and assure him that it will never happen again. My dad also told me to prepare my heart for Mr. James deciding Monica and I can't be together. My mom decided she would take Nick out so he won't be able to eavesdrop.

When Mr. James arrives, I'm sitting in the den waiting for him and my father. This is serious because we are all huge NFL fans, and we are missing the game to have this talk. I honestly didn't feel like watching football yesterday or today but still, I know my father and Mr. James would be watching if we weren't here now.

"Mr. James." I reach out to shake his hand.

"Donovan, how are you?" he shockingly shakes mine in return while forcing a smile and making eye contact.

"Nervous." I wait to sit down until he does.

"You should be." He sits across from us on the sectional.

"You want anything to drink?" asks my dad.

"Your wife made sweet tea today?"

My mom makes the best sweet tea in town, better than most restaurants. It is so good Mr. James requests her to bring it to any Brown-James family get together.

After my dad takes a few sips, Mr. James downs the whole glass and goes to pour another before he begins, "I'm pretty sure you know why I'm here, Donovan."

"Yes, sir." I don't break eye contact. According to my father, punks are scared to look you in the eye, and I can't punk out with Mr. James.

"Donovan, I like you. Always considered you to be a son," Mr. James affirms.

"Yes, sir," I agree.

"Man, this is harder than I thought," Mr. James attests.

"May I say something, Mr. James?"

"Of course. I do want to know what you were thinking."

"Well, sir, I wasn't thinking clearly. I just know I love your daughter and wanted to see her. We don't have any classes together and thought it would be cool to hang out at the movies. We shouldn't have lied to you or anyone. I promise you I won't ever lie again. My parents taught me better than that."

"I appreciate it and I know your parents didn't teach you to lie. I know your father to be a man of integrity, but I also understand puberty can make you do some stupid things. Understandably, I don't trust any boy, even you, and lying didn't help matters. Have you kissed my daughter?"

"Y-y-yes, sir."

He takes another long gulp of tea while looking me in the eyes. "Monica told me last night, just testing to see if you would lie about that, too. Donovan, I'm not ready for Monica to have a boyfriend. I was trying to hold off until thirty-five but she is so pretty and got boys lying for her. I may have to wait until sixteen."

"Sixteen, LB?" my father laughs.

"Cindy laughed at me, too, but I'm not ready." Mr. James sulks while leaning back in the armed chair.

"So, what does that mean, sir?" I already know the answer.

"This thing you have with Monica is going to have to be put on hold. This is her first year in junior high and I have to keep her focused. She can't even have boys call the house until she is thirteen so maybe then we can talk about y'all being... a couple. Okay, son?"

"Mr. James, I promise you I won't lie again," I vow begging for him to give me a chance.

"Donovan, please know you being a male is the reason why I don't trust you. I know there are some good guys out there. Your dad was and still is one of them, but my mind goes back to how I was when I was your age. Just give me some time to deal with all this. This is my babygirl, my only girl, and I'm not ready for her to grow up. Her mom is trying to help me but I ain't ready. You'll understand one day when you have a daughter."

"No offense, sir" desperation has boosted my confidence on a stupid high and I continue to say, "but it sounds like I'm not like you. I would try to give the young man some trust."

"Well, you took trust when you kissed my daughter twice without me knowing and lied about the movies," he says trying to keep his voice down.

How does he know about the second time? Technically, it has been maybe five or six times if you count yesterday. Doesn't really matter. If we only kissed once, he would still be mad.

"LB, calm down. Listen to Donovan for a minute," my dad steps in. "I understand he did lie, but do you somewhat understand why? It doesn't make it right, but you brag about popping a cap in anyone who touches your daughter. That shows D really likes or loves this girl if he is willing to risk his life to kiss her."

"Maybe he is just stupid and too young for love," Mr. James retorts.

"LB, I get that you are upset but you won't disrespect Donovan like that. You know he is smart, which is why he is attracted to your daughter who is also smart. What boy wouldn't want to go out with her?"

"That is the problem, Marcus. I can't stop dudes from liking her, but I can stop them from hanging with her, sneaking to the movies with her and having any contact with her. I got eyes at Alice Drive so they will let me know if anyone gets too close." He stares directly at me.

"Your decision is final on Donovan and Monica?" my dad presses.

"I said on hold... pause, man. I didn't say take the tape out and break it in half."

"You right. D, it could have been worse," my dad shakes my shoulder.

I don't feel any better.

No he isn't banning me from seeing her but h e is pretty much giving me a year away from my girl. I know it will be different how we hang, and to see her daily without being able to hold her hand, carry her books, kiss those lips.

I don't want to say the Lord doesn't answer prayers, but he didn't give me what I wanted. If he could change Paul's heart from killing Christians to loving them, surely, he could have changed Mr. James's heart. I guess I can be glad he didn't try to choke me out in my home, but this hurts just as much.

Actually, it is worse.

CHAPTER 12

STUBBORN MEN

Monica James

Mortified. Embarrassed. Humiliated. Flustered. Trippin'. Buggin'. All of these words are doing backflips in my stomach.

Only a few people know about this horrendous event, Nicole, Will, and I wouldn't be surprised if the boys tell Lou. My mom says this will be a story I will laugh about within a few years or even later down the road with my kids, but I just can't see it.

"Hey, kids, my first relationship was broken up by your Grandpa LB! Hardy har har!"

After crying my eyes out, I want to scream again into my pillow and blow snot into fifty more rags. How can Daddy do this to me? I know for a fact D isn't getting it as bad as me. I'm on phone punishment, and can't leave my house for at least a month due to lying to Daddy.

Not just Daddy. I lied to both of my parents.

If my daddy wasn't adamant about keeping me boyfriend free forever, my mom would have been down for supervised nights out for the pre-teens. What was crazier was hearing D wanted to meet with him. He wouldn't tell me what he and D discussed but I overheard him talking to my mom.

"I do wish there could have been a compromise, Lawrence," my mom says while folding clothes in the family room outlined with framed photographs of family and friends and Black art.

"I didn't kill him." My father throws his hands up then goes back to flipping through the channels hoping tv will distract my mom.

"Lawrence!" my mom beckons, fluffing a shirt so hard it pops loudly in the air. "The two kids like each other."

"As much as I don't care or even want to know, y'all are acting like I told them never. At least I moved my age down from 35 to 13."

After rolling her eyes, my mom argues, "No, you are just buying yourself some time. When did you have your first girlfriend?"

"That is beside the point, Cynthia. Boys just want one thing at this stage."

"That is exactly the point. You think Donovan is like you! You know all boys aren't the same, but I refuse to argue with you. Once your mind is set, I know there is no changing it despite how other people in the situation *feel* about it." She fluffs out another piece of clothing that pops loudly through the house.

"They'll get over it."

"They are not the only ones who are looking at you like you are unreasonable, Lawrence."

"I know and I don't care! A man has to stand his ground! And sometimes he has to do it alone."

My mom is curious about Mr. Marcus's reaction, which is reflecting the same attitude as my mom. He also doesn't see what the big deal is. He understands that D is as innocent as me. Dad is being unreasonable. He is acting like kids don't make mistakes. We are sometimes put into awkward situations because our parents are being too strict. Mom is desperately trying to get him to see there is nothing wrong with our feelings for each other. We are two pre-teens who have allowed their hearts to make decisions that don't make any sense. She reminds him they have all been there, but Dad ain't trying to hear it. My balloon of hope just pops, and I go back to my room to cry my eyes out some more.

The next morning my mother comes in extra early, which doesn't seem early because I must have cried myself to sleep. I normally don't get up until six but she is in there a quarter to six to place cucumbers over my eyes. She doesn't even bring up yesterday, she just tells me to lay there until she comes to get me, which seems like forever. I keep assuring myself no one else knows so it is not like I will be the laughing stock of the school. I have a feeling that Lou knows, but he wouldn't rat us out. Nevertheless, I can't forget seeing Daliyah prancing in the theater on a mission after we left.

At least one happy couple survived the first date disaster, Will and Nicole. I don't think Will deserves her. She could do better than that cheapskate who didn't have money for snacks. And I don't know how I would feel if a guy liked my girl then moved on to me. Granted, it was a short stay but he acted like on the first day of school D was a fool for not stepping to me and he wouldn't make that mistake. Interesting turn of events.

It's the second week of junior high and I wonder how I will survive my first meltdown. How will I walk through the halls and pretend my heart isn't aching? I finally get the nerve to tell D yes and my dad takes him away from me because he is too nervous his past will resurrect with his daughter. I need him to have faith in me.

"You're going to be okay, Monica," my mom says, taking the cucumbers off my eyes. I'm all cried out so I just nod. I don't feel like eating much breakfast, so I take a banana and a juice pouch to go.

My dad isn't normally up this early so I'm surprised to see him waiting outside for me. Usually, if he is up, he is reading the newspaper at the kitchen table. This morning he is sitting on the step outside of our front door. I'm glad he is dressed in jogging pants and a t-shirt rather than boxers and a t-shirt.

"Good morning, Babygirl," my dad hums while standing then pulling me into his embrace.

"Good morning, Daddy," I mumble.

"I came to talk to you last night, but you were knocked out." He kisses me on the top of my head.

"That's what crying will do to you," I huff breaking from his embrace and start walking toward my bus stop.

"I deserve that but one day you will understand." He follows behind me.

I stop and finally face him. "Donovan is not like the boys you rant and rave about. You know his boys clown him because he has never made a move on me?"

My dad just looks baffled then utters, "I didn't know."

"If he wanted to do what y'all... Honestly, it is just you who thinks some of the kids do at our age... which is disgusting... don't you think... Never mind. It's not fair." I start back walking toward my bus stop.

"This isn't the first or last time you will tell me or your mother that, Babygirl." He walks a little faster to catch up to me then pulls me back into his embrace.

"Lucky me," I say sarcastically.

My father stops me and makes me face him again, "Babygirl, it isn't the end of the world. I love you. I'm only looking out for what is best for you. I know boys are going to like you but this whole boyfriend thing and sneaking off to the movies… You're only twelve.. You're my Babygirl—"

"Dad, I get it," I interrupt him. "My bus is coming. I will see you this afternoon, okay?" I briefly make eye contact and look ahead toward the bus.

"Can your daddy get a kiss goodbye?" His eyes are pleading for me to understand and kiss him goodbye.

Grudgingly, I kiss him on the cheek and hug him goodbye. I think he detects I'm still mad because he is looking sad but changes his face to look serious when the bus arrives. I wave at him as I get on the bus and he waves back. As I walk back to my seat, I hear some of the kids laugh that my dad had to walk me to the bus stop. Little do they know, I'd rather them laugh at me about him escorting me to the bus stop than about what my father did to devastate me this weekend.

"Yo, you okay?" Nicole pulls me into her seat when I attempt to sit across from her.

"Do I look okay?" I whisper.

"I knew he would ground you but something worse happened, didn't it?" She crouches close to me.

"Dad said D and I can't be together until next year." I wipe away a tear.

"Wow!" she yells, then she brings her voice back down to a whisper, "I'm so sorry, Monica. Do you think it would have mattered if we were upfront with your parents?"

"Let's be real. My dad never would have allowed me to even go if he knew. Or worse, my parents would have made us bring our brothers."

"True, true so what are you going to do?" Nicole is checking herself out in her compact mirror then holds it up like she is noticing something behind her.

"Go back to how I was last week, acting like D and I don't exist."

"You may be acting a little dramatic. Your moms are best friends."

"I know." I lean back.

"Do you? You are acting like y'all aren't going to be homies anymore." Nicole then turns around. "Excuse me, can I help you?"

I turn around to see who she is speaking to. It's Miss Gossip Princess also known as Yolanda, better known as Daliyah's new flunky.

"I'm good. Y'all don't know how to whisper," Yolanda retorts.

"You just mind your business," Nicole shot back then turns to me. "And you were saying?"

I share my frustration, while trying to make my voice lower, about how I know things will definitely be different between D and I since my dad knows we like each other and we kissed. Hanging out will not be the same but she's trying to cheer me up because Daddy said we could possibly go steady in eighth grade. That is an improvement from age thirty-five.

"What if D ends up falling for another girl and forgets about me?" I pout.

"This boy kisses you knowing your father is supposedly trigger happy with any boy who gets with his daughter? C'mon, Monica. And he stood up to him. He isn't going anywhere. Don't start trippin' and slapping any girls over him, either. He's coming back to you. He probably has a calendar where he is marking off the days before he asks you to be his girlfriend *again.* Maybe he will propose with a ring pop." We are both tickled by the thought of him on his knees with my favorite flavor, raspberry. "Just gotta be patient, sweetie."

"I don't think she should be patient. Donovan Brown is a hot commodity," Yolanda cheers from behind us.

"Who is talking to you?" Nicole barks.

"I'm just telling the truth. Daliyah and I hung out with him at the movies Saturday."

"Why are you lying?" Nicole heckles.

I know for a fact Daliyah and Yolanda were there but I know Donovan didn't hang with them. He wouldn't betray me like that.

"Monica, you better keep Big D under wraps. That is all I'm saying." She starts checking herself out in her compact mirror.

Never have I been someone to get caught up in drama or fight over a boy. Yet, I'm fuming like she has one more crazy thing to say before I knock her upside her head.

When the bus driver stops to let more kids on, Nicole grabs me and we sit as far away as possible to avoid any more drama. Moving gets us fussed out by the bus driver but it's worth it. Yolanda is messy like Daliyah.

While trying to get it together, I wonder if my dad will stay true to his word or push back the boyfriend age limit to sixteen. Given how sad he looked today, I doubt it. Maybe he will change his mind and not make D and me wait but that is truly wishful thinking.

Thankfully, I don't have any classes with him and only see him at recess. We don't even pass each other unless we are going to our homerooms or afternoon dismissal. It was like God knew this would happen. Seeing D would be unbearable. While he's at it, I need Him to work on my father's heart and melt it or something. As my grandmother would scream out in church, *touch him, Lord.*

What is unavoidable are the rumors circulating around that D broke up with me to be with Daliyah. Why am I being tested? As much as I want to confront the rumors, I can't. I told my mom I could handle the drama of middle school. Granted, I didn't think it would happen this quickly. Don't these kids have homework to do or quizzes to study for? Why are they worrying about me and D?

At recess, I want to talk to D, but he is too busy playing basketball. Will, Lou, and he brought a quick change of clothes, so they won't mess up their gear. I refuse to look like I'm waiting for him. I just join the Double Dutch crew.

This goes on for the whole week like he is avoiding me. Boys are so stupid. What is crazier is I think the rumors are true. You love me but you can't talk to me, even say hi or deny the lies of Daliyah. Then I remember one of my dad's fraternity brothers works here, and D knows it. Ironically, he supervises our recess. His name is Charles Geddis or Mr. G. Could Dad have asked him to make sure we don't hang out?

Wanting to believe it is a coincidence, the James and Brown families don't see each other for weeks. Between our brothers' sports schedules and going out of town for family matters, there is no time for our normal outings or evening dinners. Nicole, who I call Nikki since we solidified that we are best friends, and I both believe our moms are just buying time for things to cool down between Mr. Brown and my dad. I think my dad rubbed Mr. Marcus the wrong way. I heard he called D stupid and Mr. Marcus called him on it. Supposedly, he apologized but I still can't believe Daddy would be so rude.

Keeping my head above the waves of drama that seem to be approaching low tide, I'm ready to blow off some steam at my first junior high dance. We are getting ready at my house but we are having a slumber party at Nikki's house.

"You excited about the dance tonight?" Nikki asks again while adding some more curls to her already curly do.

"My answer hasn't changed from the first time you asked me," I reply, staring in the vanity in my bedroom with her while trying to figure out if I want to change my hair for the fifth time.

"C'mon, Moni Love, your parents are letting you off punishment a week early so you can go. You gotta be excited."

I crack a smile. "Trust me, I want to be excited but I know D will be there. Honestly, he may avoid me like he has been doing for the past few weeks. Maybe I should wear a ponytail with my bang."

"I heard Demetrius has a crush on you," she starts fluffing out her curls.

"Why are you giving me another name to turn down?" I pull my hair down out of the ponytail.

"So you just going to be dateless at Alice Drive until your boy is allowed to come around?" She rolls her eyes.

"Yes… I guess… I don't know. Demetrius is cute," I giggle, "but a part of me feels like I'm playing D."

"Child, please. You already know girls—" She stops because I'm shooting her red glares.

"Please don't remind me. Every chick wants him, including Daliyah." I snatch a black, velvet bucket hat to cover my hair because I can't decide how to style it.

As much as I'm certain D isn't going to go for Daliyah, it still agitates me. Why is she even trying to mack him? He doesn't pay her any attention. I heard about the notes she passes to him that he throws in the trash. I think she tries so hard to aggravate me, maybe to knock me off my game because we will eventually compete for the top spots on the track team in the spring. I still owe her for the last fiasco.

I'm no longer angry at my father. I had to let it go. I have forgiven him, although I still don't understand the waiting period. D surely doesn't mind other girls hollering at him so maybe I should holla back at someone like Demetrius.

Finally, we make it to the dance and I'm surprised we can see. My mom's flash on her camera would cause any man to go blind. I wish she wouldn't bug out over moments like this, but she wouldn't be a Mom if she didn't.

My mom has offered to drop my bag at Nikki's house after she drops off her camera film at the drugstore. Nikki's mom said to make sure she gets double prints of the pictures we took together   .

Before going into the gym, we head straight into the girls' restroom where we are hyping each other over our cute outfits like we didn't get ready together. We are both rocking acid wash overalls, Looney Tune characters posed like TLC, and combat boots. She mentions when all the other girls leave the restroom that D wants to dance with me. While containing my excitement, I guarantee that D will have to wait in line behind the other fellas who are not afraid to speak to me.

"I see you playing hard to get! You better make D put in work for acting like a jerk the last few weeks!" We high five each other.

When D tried to approach me, another guy would come and sweep me up. It is hard because D looks so cute tonight with his Karl Kani gear on. He has a fresh cut, too. Luckily, I sneak peeks without him noticing.

Finally, I break away from another dance with Demetrius by convincing him I need a break. He offers me some punch, but I lie and say I'm not thirsty.

Nikki comes to my rescue and pulls me into the inner circle I used to belong to: Will, Lou, and D.

"Look who I found!" Nikki yells over the music.

"Oh, hey, Monica," D says, acting uninterested.

Really? This is the game he wants to play?

"Long time, no see," I say nonchalantly, playing along with him.

"How you been?" He is not even making eye contact.

"Been good. You?" I stare at him proving I can be mature.

"Chilling." He briefly makes eye contact.

An awkward silence takes over, which is accompanied by a slow song leaving us two standing alone since everyone is dancing with someone on the dance floor.

Demetrius looks like he wants to make his way across the dance floor, but D finally asks, "You want to dance?" He is looking into my eyes for the first time, and I can't help but forget about the jerk who took over his body.

To be in his arms right now is heaven and takes me back to the last time I kissed those soft lips. I must blink my eyes to stop watering because I see I'm not over him.

He pulls me close then starts talking in my ear, "I miss you."

"D, with all those girls you been macking…"

"Those girls aren't you, MJ, and you know it," he interrupts and we immediately stop dancing. "No one compares to you. I love you."

I blink back more tears then fold my arms in disgust. "You know how I feel about you, D, but you also know what my father said."

"I don't care anymore. It's been a month and I think we should go back to him. Tell him to let up." He pulls me close to him then, hugging me around my neck. His lips are so close to me but I can't… I won't fall back out of my father's good graces again.

"Are you trying to die?" I'm hoping to talk sense into D. I know eyes are on us but I can't back away.

"For you, I will. I'm so sick of playing this game. You don't think I'm watching you at recess? I only play ball to get distracted from watching you. Now Demetrius trying to holla—"

"So, Demetrius has you wanting me back?" I back away.

"No, not having you, MJ, has me wanting you back." He pulls me back into his embrace.

My father is the reason I'm at this dance tonight. My mom even told me not to rush him in his decision. D's cologne is trying to sway me but I just can't.

"I miss you, too, but we can't, D."

"Don't you want to be with me?" His arms around me loosen but don't let go.

"You heard what my dad said." Why is he pressing me? This isn't even like him. He is one of the most patient people I know.

While still holding back tears, I want to mean mug him, but I see Daliyah watching our every move. He pulls away and looks at me like I just stabbed him in the heart. I'm a daddy's girl. It isn't worth it.

"Either you love me or you don't. It's either now or never, Monica." He completely let me go.

"You're giving me an ultimatum?" I scoff.

"Good night, Monica." He kisses me on the forehead then walks away.

This can't be happening. Did I lose D forever? Why is he being so freaking stubborn?

"Are you okay?" Demetrius breaks me from my thoughts. *Where did he come from?*

"Ummm, yeah. My nose won't stop running so I need to go to the restroom," I lie. I can't cry in front of these people, especially Daliyah.

"Cool, I'll be waiting for you," Demetrius calls behind me.

I force a smile then run into the restroom not realizing Nikki is following me. I explain what happened with D and she flips. I get her being mad, but she is straight trippin'.

"Chill out, Nikki!" I'm trying to keep her in the restroom.

"Chill out? Chill out my butt. I wanted y'all back together, too, but not like that. Who does he think he is?" She keeps trying to march toward the door to leave but I snatch her back in.

"I need you to calm down. He said he loves me and really—"

"What does love have to do with it? Love doesn't do that. Get yourself together. I'm going to jack up Will's behind. I know he knew!"

"What? Will? What about D? Hold up, what are you going to do?" I wipe my face and blow my nose once more, which gives her a clearing to exit with a rage I don't understand.

"Break up with his sorry butt. Why would he agree to something like that… and he lied to me! He said D just wanted to dance."

Before I can talk sense into her, Nikki confronts Will about D giving me an ultimatum. This doesn't make sense. She should be confronting D. She feels like Will knew and should have warned her or talked sense into him. D attempts to calm her down by stepping between Will and her and gets his head cut off. Immediately, the teacher chaperones come over and Nikki pulls a 180, calmly breaks up with Will, and then saunters into the gym like nothing happened.

I can't believe that just happened. She is blowing this way out of proportion. I don't think Will knew. Maybe he did know but Nikki didn't have to break up with her boo over D and me but it does prove this chick is my BFF for life.

Before I can follow my best friend back into the gym, I see Daliyah grinning with a satisfaction that I wish I could snatch off her face.

CHAPTER 13

MOVING ON

Monica James

—

Rayshon ends up picking us up from the dance and I'm surprised Nikki isn't opening her mouth about what happened. She is pissed about what was supposed to be a super dope night. I think Rayshon suspects it, so she speaks to me first while eyeing Nikki in the rearview mirror.

"Monica, how was the dance?" she chirps trying to lighten up the mood. It is obvious Nikki isn't trying to talk to anyone.

"It was cool," I remark looking at Nikki.

"Nikki, you sure you don't want to talk about it?" Rayshon presses.

After an awkward silence and a long sigh, Nikki finally comments, "Boys are stupid!"

"Tell me something I don't know," Rayshon laughs. "I guess you and Will broke up tonight?"

"He lied to me, Shon. You know how I feel about lying."

"Yeah, I know. What did he lie about?" Rayshon inquires.

"He made it seem like D just wanted to dance with Monica tonight and D ends up giving Monica some now or never crap..."

"An ultimatum?" Rayshon gawks at us.

"Yeah!" Nikki throws her hands up.

"Y'all are in seventh grade. What y'all know about that? Sounding like an episode of *The Young and the Restless*," Rayshon jests.

"Either way, I know Will knew and he didn't tell me. He knows I wouldn't be down for that!"

"Will told you he knew?" Rayshon feels the same confusion I do about Nikki's anger.

"No, but I know he did," Nikki is adamant about his betrayal.

"You still don't know if he knew," I finally speak up.

"What?" Nikki attests, "I know he knew."

"What if he didn't know, Nikki?" Rayshon tries to reason with her.

"I don't care. He called me crazy."

"*What?* Now no one is allowed to call you crazy except me and maybe Monica." We all cackle at Rayshon's joke. It's good to see Nikki smiling again.

"He was starting to get on my nerves, anyway, and I heard Tyasia was making a play for him and he was playing back," Nikki huffs.

— "Yeah, I heard that, too, but I knew you would handle it," I add.

"Through your words," Rayshon commands, "We are not going down that road again, Nikki!"

"Yes, Mama Shon," Nikki jokes.

I love watching the two of them together. It makes me want an older sister like her. She is right that Nikki doesn't need to go back to the fighting, which is why she is over here at Alice Drive.

When I first met her, it was hard to believe she was or is a fighter. But the way she almost knocked Will and D's head off made it believable. I heard the stories, but she said she only got buck with those who got buck with her. In other words, she didn't beat up random people. Beating up anyone isn't okay. She said she was provoked like Will supposedly provoked her tonight. I'm still not understanding exactly how. Based on his reaction, I don't think Will knew what D was going to do. Nevertheless, I'm glad she stopped herself from tearing off his head to keep herself out of trouble.

Even if he did, it isn't Will's job to control D. She has to know that. The girl is super smart. The only way my parents let her come over when I was on punishment was to tutor me when I'm struggling in a subject. She makes A's easily and I have been struggling to maintain them.

"This is y'all's first junior high dance. I hope what D told you didn't jack up your whole night. Nikki told me how much y'all like each other."

"I'll get over him. If he loves me like he says he does, he wouldn't have done that tonight. I don't even know who he is anymore. Who forces someone to go against their parents? That wasn't my D," I sigh and then change the subject. "Demetrius did look extra cute tonight, and he has a twin sister. She can call the house asking for me so we can talk."

"Girl, I'm pretty sure your parents can tell if you are on the phone with a boy versus a girl."

"Haven't thought about it but it is worth a try."

"Don't end up on lockdown again, Little Miss Missy," Rayshon laughs.

"I won't… I won't."

We finally make it to their home and I'm so thankful she let her company shower first. I hate feeling like a hot sticky mess in someone else's house. After we both shower, I was so happy to see her mom has pizza, popcorn, and soda in her room with trays to eat them on. I'm hungry, and something else started bothering me.

"Did you see Daliyah and Tyasia talking to Donovan?"

My mind flashes back to Daliyah strutting over to D in the gym after I chased Nicole inside. Her favorite song came on so she dragged me onto the dance floor. I kept looking through the gym doors, which was hard. Maybe I was seeing things but it looked like she was cracking up with Donovan, Will, and Lou. It was her, Yolanda, and Tyasia, who is rumored to like Will.

"Hold up, Tyasia was kicking it with Daliyah?" she questions.

"Yeah," from her tone I regret telling her.

She chews unnecessarily hard on popcorn. "Your boy was trippin' tonight but I don't think he is a backstabber. Now, Will… That wanna be player was probably ready to move on," Nikki huffs while popping more popcorn in her mouth. "I see the way he looks at her."

"This is the same boy who was giving you the stare down in class and then was asking for my digits during recess. I told you I didn't like Will."

She huffs and pops more popcorn in her mouth.

"But I do think there is something more to this than you are letting on," I turn the TV down.

She is still munching hard on popcorn.

"You my girl, but you are seriously freaking out over nothing. So what, D wanted to act like a jack butt today? If you feeling 'ol dude, don't jack it up based on what you think you saw or heard."

"What if I already did?" Nicole stuffs her mouth with more popcorn.

"So what are you going to do?" I take a slow sip of my soda.

She does the same then lets out a loud belch. She wipes her mouth with a napkin, and doesn't excuse herself. "What I'm not going to do is apologize. After I showed my behind, I'm not eating any humble pie."

"There are too many dudes at Alice Drive for you to be sad over Will." I high five her.

"I'll get over him, but look who's talking?" Nikki retorts.

"What?" I hesitate.

"You can front with Shon, but you forgot I was in the restroom with you."

"Yeah, it hurts but let's be real, boys are stupid but not all boys. I think Demetrius may be one of the smart ones."

"You were just saying how you weren't trying to feel anyone else but D and now you are all about Demetrius?"

"I need you to stop trippin' and twistin' my words. I'm willing to give another brother some play after D showed his behind tonight." I attempt to cheer Nikki up by stating, "I heard Marcell has been checking you out."

"Marcell Bivens?"

"Eighth grader... Marcell!"

"Ooooookay!" We both erupt in laughter then finish our food.

Now I think I kind of see why my dad didn't want me to have a boyfriend because he knew they all had the potential to break your heart like D did tonight. I just can't understand what has gotten into him. I heard hormones make pre-teens and teens do some foolish things, but the hormones can't be raging so much that D forgot who he was dealing with.

D and I are on the same level and best friends, or at least I thought we were. Who gives their best friend an ultimatum? Seriously? It is not like this is a life-or-death situation. He is being selfish, and I can't call someone my best friend if he is acting selfishly. Then to add more stank to this situation I saw him laughing with Daliyah.

What is this world coming to?

POETIC INTERMISSION

Monica James

Out of Tune

The one guy I thought
I could give my heart to
wants me to choose between
right and wrong.
Right is my choice
Yet, I'm the one
humming the tune of a heartbreak song entitled
"I told you."
The record keeps spinning.
Daddy is the DJ.
Most importantly,
feeling uneasy.
Rhythm, beat, rhyme is unfamiliar.
Harmony has evaded us.
Discord has come between us.
How after twelve years
we can't find the beat
that will put us back in sync?

CHAPTER 14

REGRETS

Donovan Brown

The car ride with Will, Lou, and me is eerily quiet. We would only speak to my pops but not to each other. I don't know if it's because we are trying to figure out what the heck just happened. It isn't until we are playing video games in the playroom that I finally speak up.

"What the heck happened tonight?" I exclaim.

"Both of us lost our girls for good!" Will threw down his remote after we both got killed in the game. "What the heck did you say to Monica?"

"I had to check her, told her now or never," I boast.

Will and Lou both gawk at me like I'm speaking another language. I explain how it has been frustrating not being able to be with the girl I love.

"You can't deny what the heart wants," Lou shocks the heck out of all of us with his sentimental gibberish. Will and I both look at him like he turned into an alien.

"What? I know I'm the mack of the group, but a playa knows true love when I see it. People say we are too young for it, which is why I don't deal with it. Chicks will flip in a minute over the stupidest stuff!"

"Whatever, Lou. D, it's jacked up her dad has a freaking spy so you can't really step to her like you want to, but making her choose between her father and you is jacked up, too. I thought playing basketball was taking your mind off her, and then you approach her with this," Will attempts to understand.

"It doesn't even matter anymore," I reassure my homies.

"Don't play yourself!" Lou stresses.

"Just like that you're giving up… just because she won't give you what you want?" Will reasons.

"I get you been sweating this girl since forever, but come on, D," Lou adds.

"I got tired of waiting," I plead.

Why don't they understand?

It was different when I couldn't see her every day. Seeing her everyday looking as fine as she does is killing me softly. Imagine being told you can have your favorite piece of candy, cake or any sweet treat. Then the person who is giving it to you tells you that you are not ready to eat it. Instead of taking it away, they just let it sit on the table. The amount of torture you have to endure on a daily basis is relentless.

Will throws a pillow at me. "You acting like her father said you could never speak to Monica again. Maybe Nicole hit you when she took a swing at me. You not making sense."

"Straight buggin'," Lou snorts. "You gotta go see that girl when your families visit."

"I can ask to stay at your place," I point at Will. Lou would be an option if he wasn't moving. His dad got stationed in Panama City, Florida, so we decided to have a sleepover before he heads out tomorrow.

"Your moms will go for that?" Will questions.

Lou just shakes his head like he is ashamed of his homeboy. Yeah, I'm punking out but it will lessen the sting of this heartache.

"It is worth a try, dog. What happened with you and Nicole?" I try to change the subject.

Everyone has heard the stories about Nicole and how she is Mike Tyson with any chick who wants to test her. If I can't be with the girl I love, maybe I can help Will get his girl back.

Will shatters my plan when he mentions that he is ready to give Tyasia a chance. We have all seen the notes she passes that he doesn't answer. We all agree that Tyasia is fine. She isn't Monica fine, but she is pleasing to the eye. Will said he isn't a playa so once he is talking to someone, he only talks to them.

You can tell he was really feeling Nicole, but can't understand why she flipped the way she did. None of us can. Lou and I both wonder if

Nicole gave into the rumor mill. Some believed that Daliyah broke up me and Monica, which I squashed with anyone who stepped to me with that foolishness. Lou and I are not surprised that Nicole probably heard Tyasia hyping up a love connection between her and Will when we all know there isn't one. It really doesn't matter because Nicole revealed a side of her that Will can't get past

Before we can discuss the issue any further, my father is knocking on the door.

"Fellas, I'm just checking on you before I turn in," my father peeks in.

"Mr. Brown, I need your advice for a friend or two," Lou brings someone else into our business.

My pops wonders what he walked into. He trudges in after looking at his watch. You can tell he was just checking in and he wasn't expecting to give advice. Will and I really want to bop Lou upside his head. We got this handled. Because my father is dope and believes in being there for his family and people who are like family, he is not going to ask if this can wait until breakfast.

"What's up?" he sits on the couch behind us.

"Okay, my friend—" Lou faces my dad.

"Lou, it is too late for you to be lying about your friend. Is it you, Will or Donovan?"

"Maybe I should have told you the problem has to do with girls. Mr. Brown, girls have never been an issue with me," he pats himself on the chest. "I got my game on lock." Lou has us rolling, laughing at his confused confidence. "What are y'all laughing at? Y'all want to fall in love. I ain't got time for that!"

"Yeah, you too busy being a knucklehead playa'," my father comments while hitting on the back of his head with a pillow.

"Whatever, Mr. Brown. I don't know why you have to clown a brother when he is reaching out on the behalf of your sons," Lou points to us.

"I don't want to talk to my father about this!" I mumble avoiding eye contact with my father or anyone for that matter.

"Whatever. I will talk about me but you need to talk to your pops!" Will throws a pillow at me.

"Fellas, my bed is calling me," my dad looks at his watch again.

"Mr. James, I like my girl, but she was trippin' off something she thought was going on and it wasn't," Will admits.

"Did you try to talk to her about it?" my dad questions.

"I couldn't. hhe was straight trippin'! Trying to fight over something she heard. She didn't give me time to explain," Will counters.

"Then move on, son, unless you like this girl a lot," my dad concludes.

"She is fine, but she isn't the only fine one at Alice Drive," Lou adds.

"I didn't ask if she is fine. I asked if you liked her a lot."

Will gives him a blank stare.

"Y'all too young to get hung up on one girl, but if you really like someone then you are willing to work it out. If you don't like her like that, which I think you do because you are asking me for advice, then move on," Dad reiterates.

"But you didn't move on with Mom," I remind Dad.

"Now you want to talk about this?" My dad pauses and I finally make eye contact with him. "I told you your mom and me and you and Monica are different. LB told you to wait until next year so what is the issue?"

"Your son gave her an ultimatum tonight," Lou mocks.

My dad just gapes at me and tries to hold his laughter in but howls at my pain. Is my dad really clowning me right now?

"Dad?" I throw a pillow at him.

"You the one sounding like Neil from *Young and the Restless*," he chokes through laughter. Finally he stops to get serious for a quick second, "I taught you better than that, son."

"This fool hasn't been listening." Will points and rolls over in laughter on his back.

"I love her, and she needs to make a decision," I reason.

"You're asking your best friend, who is technically still a child, to side with a young man who is acting like a selfish, spoiled brat." He pauses to let those words sting my ego. "You acting like a year is forever. You should be grateful LB gave you that much."

"Dad, you forget I go to school with her? I have to see her when they visit or we visit."

"You never heard the quote 'If you love something and have to let it go if it is meant to be... it will come back?'"

"Yeah, but I'm not trying to hear that," I huff.

"You're so love sick you are delusional and impatient, son."

"Don't forget selfish, Mr. Brown," Lou calls out.

Will agrees along with my pops who questions, "You are willing to toss twelve years of friendship out of the window?"

"If she loves me, she would remember those twelve years," I huff again.

"Do you hear yourself? It is not about y'all or what works best for both of you. You're not even meeting her halfway. It is all about you."

I just hunch my shoulders.

"What would you do?" Will questions my father.

"I would apologize to her to try to salvage anything y'all have left," my father stares at me.

"She should understand," I reason still not getting it.

"Think about if the situation was flipped? How would you feel if Monica tried to come between you and me or you and your mom? Despite how crazy LB is, the man is close to his daughter. Monica will always be a daddy's girl and boys come a dime a dozen, son."

"I'm not just some boy, Dad," I plead.

"You don't think I know this, son, but you acted like some random boy tonight. You didn't act like the boy or young man who respects his girl and her decision to respect her father. You acted like those chumps who are—"

"Like I said, *selfish!*" Lou repeats.

Dad is looking at Lou like he doesn't need his help but is somewhat shocked Lou is making sense.

My dad doesn't fake the funk for anyone including his oldest son, who feels like a freaking idiot.

What did I do?

I want to make this right, but I feel like Monica isn't going to hear anything I have to say. I told her now or never and if I go back on what I said it will make me seem like a punk or I don't know what I want. But I'm supposed to be her best friend so I should have cared about what her father said. Why is love so freaking confusing?

"You finally see the light," Dad reacts to the regret written all over my face.

I fall back into the couch, speechless. My dad just shakes his head and then gives Will and Lou dap on his way out. I heard love makes you do stupid things. I look real stupid right now.

Everyone is encouraging me to apologize.

I *know* I should apologize.

What Will and Lou don't understand is I don't think Monica is going to make it that easy.

CHAPTER 15

AWKWARD SPACE

Monica James

Besides recess, I haven't seen D in three weeks. I know he is avoiding me, which makes me wonder if he feels sorry for acting like a jack butt. When his parents come over, they say D is over at Will's. D has never skipped out on a trip to see his second family.

To make matters worse, he has been real chummy with Daliyah. No, I can't tell him who to like but Daliyah? Nicole doesn't think he likes her. According to her, he's just being friendly. We don't befriend the enemy. That isn't like D.

None of this is.

Speaking of Will, Nikki and him never made up. He never apologized, although it should be the other way around. Nikki has been Marcell's girl for the past three weeks. In our electives, we have classes with other grade levels, so they have art together and he lives in her neighborhood.

They make a cute couple but not as cute as her and Will. I know that sounds crazy coming from me when I didn't think Will was cute enough and a straight up bum. Again, he showed up to the movies with no money. It is hard to put my finger on it, but her and Marcell don't click like her and Will did. I'm not trying to tell her because she isn't trying to admit she misses Will.

Will and Tyasia are hanging in there and it doesn't help that they have classes together and some of those classes are with Nicole. If I   think about it, I think that is why D has been chummy with Daliyah who is best friends with Tyasia.

Can they not have a girlfriend who isn't friends with their homie's girlfriend?

During the three weeks of D's hiatus, my dad comes to me in my room and asks, "What is going on with you and D?"

Ever since Dad painted the room lavender, he's periodically come in to marvel at the awesome job he did. My lavender room holds all white furniture from the desk and chair to the dresser. Next to one of my twin beds is one of my two bookshelves but this one doesn't have any books. It holds my mini stereo system and multiple cassette tapes, like Mary J Blige's *What's the 411?* Missing my best friend got me listening to "Reminisce" over and over to the point I had to ask my mom to take me to Camelot to buy another cassette tape.

I slide my headphones off then turn off my music and just give him a weird look.

"Did I say something wrong?" He is confused at my reaction.

"When have you ever been concerned about me and D, Dad?" I move my book bag out of the desk chair.

"Y'all were attached at the hip," my dad takes a seat in the chair, propping up his feet on my bed.

"Comfortable?" I snort.

"What is up with the attitude?" Surprisingly, he's looking confused rather than agitated, which is my parents' normal response when I mouth off.

"Dad, did you forget D and I became unattached when you told us not to be together? But you were right, Daddy. Boys are stupid."

"What did D do?" he throws his hand up.

"So you can go load your gun, Daddy?" I ask, trying to figure out why he wants to know.

"I need y'all to stop thinking I'm going to really kill the boy."

I give him the *who you kidding* look.

"Babygirl, he is my godson so maybe I will put him in a headlock, but—"

"Daddy." I throw a pillow at him while trying to keep myself from smiling.

"You don't have to hide your beautiful smile. Seriously, what did D do?" He tucks the pillow behind his back. "I didn't think y'all would fall out as friends. I want to make sure you are okay. I see the look in your eyes when you find out D isn't here. I know you miss him. Can a daddy be concerned about his babygirl?"

"Yes, but I will be okay." I stand from the bed to hug him and kiss him on the forehead then plop myself on his lap.

"Why won't you tell me?" he presses.

"I'm afraid. I don't think you will kill him, but I don't want you to look at him differently." I put my headphones on my stereo.

"I can be objective." Daddy sits up to look attentive.

"Pinky promise you will keep this between us." I hold out my pinky.

"Does your mom know?" he perks up.

"Nooooooo. What does that have to do with anything?" I wonder while moving back to the bed.

"You tell your mom everything. Me having a secret over your mom is like gold, Babygirl," he gloats.

Is he serious? I roll my eyes while laughing at my dad who is bouncing like a kid who found out a secret about Santa Claus.

"So your mom doesn't know about the stupid thing Donovan did? Oh, shucks now!"

I roll my eyes then hold out my pinkie closer to him. He grabs it tightly then claps his hands together like someone receiving juicy gossip. I recall the catastrophe of events that went down at our first junior high dance, which he realizes is when D started playing the *disappearing act*.

"Well, D gave me an ultimatum."

"An ulti-what?" he shrieks then bursts into uncontrollable laughter.

"Daddy, stop it and listen," I break down into giggles while trying to shush him.

"Give me a minute!" He is holding his stomach while letting the tears fall. "Whooo, that boy loves you. You're right, Babygirl. Boys can be stupid. When we love you or really like you, we don't think."

"You don't even know what the ultimatum was, Daddy," I attempt to explain.

"Oh, my bad. Him giving you an ultimatum is hilarious! Whoooo!"

"Don't go yapping your mouth with Mr. Marcus." I poke out my pinkie again.

"Y'all just having a good ol' time in here, aren't y'all?" Mom busts through the door, surprising both of us.

Dad straightens up and quickly composes himself, "Can I have a moment with my babygirl?"

"Excuse me, sir. Dinner will be ready soon." She backs slowly out of the room looking at us suspiciously. We both went from laughing to a serious face in two-point-five seconds.

We both stare at my door and wait until we hear her in the kitchen.

"You never did tell me what he said when you talked to him," I remind him.

"The boy was man enough to say I wasn't being fair. He can be trusted. He isn't like I was at his age. Blah, blah, blah. The boy poured out his heart and I called him stupid."

"Daddy," I gently shove his shoulder. "You did what?" I had heard rumors but my dad confirming it made it worse.

"I lost my cool. It was wrong. If he came by, I would have apologized by now."

"Daddy, you have a car. You could drive over there and apologize. Oh my goodness!" I lean back on the bed and cover my head with a pillow. "Hearing what you said explains his ultimatum." I sit straight up quickly.

Imitating D's voice, Dad says, "Be my tenderoni. I don't care about your father. I love you, girl!" He crosses his arms across his chest like he is a rapper.

Daddy is cracking me up. I was not expecting this conversation to bring some sunshine to my cloudy day. I assured him that D didn't mimic Bobby Brown while breaking my heart that night.

For the first time, someone notices another way I have been avoiding any sight of D since he wants to be MIA: the framed picture of me, D, and my brothers on that embarrassing day at Chuck-E-Cheese before the beat down is peeking from my desk drawer.

After Donovan didn't show up to my house after the second week, I knew he was intentionally avoiding me. That is the only picture I have of us together in my room so I couldn't look at his face in my lavender haven. Daddy pulls out the picture frame and questions if I believe the friendship is over.

"Yeah, duh, Dad! He doesn't talk to me at school. And who tries to force their best friend to do something against their parents?"

"He is your best friend who really likes, or as he would put it, loves you." He holds the frame up to prove a point. "Love makes you do stupid, desperate things. When a boy really wants to prove they love or like that special girl, foolish looks smart to them. Common sense goes out the window." I guess he doesn't want to completely impose his will so he props the frame up on the back of the desk, giving me the autonomy to hang it back up. He turns back to me and says, "Did I ever tell you the story behind the tattoo on my arm?"

Dad explains how my mom hates tattoos but, at the time, she was studying Japanese in college. He had to do something drastic to impress her and prove his playa playing days were over. The tattoo was supposed to say *she is the wind who swept me off my feet.* We're both laughing when he finally gets out it says *I love pigs feet.*

Now I'm the one laughing hysterically to the point of tears.

Without saying a word, I get up and hug my dad again. I now understand D's actions were rooted in love. I can also see that Daddy is starting to come around. I don't think this means D and I can be together, but he obviously is accepting that his babygirl is growing up and there is nothing he can do to stop it.

Honestly, at this point, even if he said we could be together, I don't want to. I will follow my father's advice and forgive him but I don't trust him. He punked out on me and best friends don't fake on each other.

Despite seeing him at recess, I couldn't walk over to speak to him. First, I didn't know if Dad still had his spy on the job. Also, I would look desperate because the rumor was that he broke up with me. He has had at least two girlfriends since the dance. Thankfully, neither of them were Daliyah, who is still trying hard to make that happen. Nicole said it is because he can't find a girl who is like me, which could be true.

Demetrius and I never worked out because he was aggravating. He would want to talk all day and night and he doesn't realize a sista gotta keep her grades up. I'm not missing out on the honor roll because he was lovesick. He would have the nerve to get mad because my mom would say it was time to get off the phone. He wanted to plan our future kids and wedding. I just couldn't deal and he wasn't into sports. I was happy it ended.

It is almost a month before I set eyes on D again at my house. I heard his parents made him come, which adds more tension in the air. My parents are out back in the sunroom while we are on the couch watching music videos in the den.

We spoke when he came in and that is all I'm willing to say. He looks cute with a fresh haircut.

Our brothers are allowed to roam the neighborhood by themselves now so they are either at the fort we built over the summer or playing with some other neighborhood kids. Now and again, I would see my mom and his mom peek in the window to see if we are talking yet. A part of me feels like they are spying on us to make sure we don't sneak a kiss again.

Man, please.

Forty-five minutes later, my mom comes back in the house and asks if D wants some more to drink and of course he accepts like he is dying of thirst. Why is she babying him like this isn't considered his house? He has always been allowed to go in the fridge and get his own drinks. I guess his shame has him stuck to the couch. All you could hear between singing, rapping, and commercials are the click of his ice cubes every time he would take another gulp.

"I'm glad someone in this house cares about my thirst," he finally mumbles after Mom left to go back with the grown people.

"You acting like you can't fix your own drink," I mumble back.

"What is wrong with you?" he retorts.

"You acting like you have been trying to talk to me this whole time. D, whatever!"

"Demetrius make you mad or something?"

"At least Demetrius isn't a big punk like you," I lie. They are both punks.

"So I'm a punk now?"

I spin around to face him so fast that I'm surprised I didn't give myself whiplash. "Having fifty million girlfriends doesn't make you the man, Donovan. Looking like a broke down Don Juan with Daliyah hanging around you like a sad puppy," I roll my neck to emphasize my point.

I'm lying about him being a broke down Don Juan. D is super cute and makes Don Juan look broke down but I refuse to blow up his ego any more than those chicks around school have.

He grabs his heart like he is Fred Sanford. MJ is his name for me and D is the name close friends and family call him. I guess I hurt his feelings. I didn't mean to or maybe I did. He hurt me. I'm not following Daddy's advice about being cool the next time I see D. To emphasize his agony, D storms off out of the house. "I'm going for a walk."

"Peace, homie," I turn up the volume to the TV.

"I'm not your homie," he huffs.

Is he straight trippin' right now? Oh, heck no. I don't even look to see if our parents are watching. I immediately jumped up to stab him more with my words.

"You got that right, Donovan Brown! A homie wouldn't act like a butt at the dance and be MIA while cheesing up in Daliyah's face." Frustration, disappointment, and anger tries to leak out of my eyes.

"What did you say?" As he is turning around to face my wrath, I push him out the storm door because I know our moms are trying to eavesdrop.

"If you weren't a girl, Monica..."

Who is this guy? Shocked and disgusted, I just gawk at him.

"You don't like how that feels?" he mocks.

"You know what, Donovan? Matter of fact, you would do what, Donovvvvvan? Instead of breaking my heart, you just punch me in it? That's what you'll do, Donovan? The D I know would never," I poke him hard in the chest, "he would never threaten any girl, especially his best friend!"

His shoulders sulk down to a level I think we have both been feeling since this rift between us. His eyes began to water then he looks away to I guess wipe his face. I turn to wipe mine. I'm not crying in front of him. I'm not giving him an opportunity to watch my heart bleed.

"I never meant to hurt you, MJ," he reaches out to me when I turn back around.

Smacking his hand away, I say, "Don't... You act like you don't see me at recess. You can't come over to the crib anymore like you hiding. Your parents had to make you come here today. Who you hiding from? You and Daliyah are going steady?"

"I've been trippin' but I ain't trippin' that hard. There is no me and Daliyah. She got the school thinking otherwise but I promise you that she could be the last girl on earth and I would have to die lonely."

That comment causes a slight smirk to appear on my face.

"I couldn't face you," he finally admits what Daddy was telling me. "I know I acted like a punk. You're supposed to be my homie and I was a jerk at the dance."

"Why couldn't you say that a month ago?" I push him in the chest.

"Maybe I didn't want to admit I messed up." He holds my hands then pulls us more out of sight of the front door.

"Hmmm, really?" I attempt to pull away.

"You can't blame a dude for wanting to be with the girl he loves." He is inching closer to me.

"D, don't throw that word around," I finally snatch my hands away. I wag my finger in his face, "You haven't spoken to me in a month."

"The fact that you realize it has been a month tells me you miss me."

I try to keep myself from blushing so I turn around so he can't see me. He is cheesing hard, so it is hard to hold it in.

"I don't know what you are talking about," I turn back around trying to keep a straight face.

"You don't have to lie *when it is written all over your face*," he starts to sing. "*You don't have to say a word*."

I never met someone who couldn't sing and loves to sing. He sounds horrible but I can't stop blushing and laughing at him.

"Shut up." I go to hit him, and he pulls me into a hug.

"Don't you realize our parents can walk around the corner at any moment?"

"I have figured out your dad isn't going to kill me. He may choke me out but won't put a cap in my behind. Being choked out because I'm hugging my girl will be worth it."

"Hold up." I break from his embrace. "Your girl?"

"Yeah, I'll break up with Shayna tonight for you."

"You don't get it," I pace back and forth in the grass to stop myself from knocking that smirk off his face. "You tried to make me pick between you and my father then I don't hear from you until now? We're just supposed to just kiss and make up?"

"Yeah." He pulls me into another hug and tries to kiss me again, but I mush his face and just stomp back into the house.

Ironically, my mom picks that moment to come back into the house to "check on us."

D is standing in the front yard looking clueless.

DISCUSSION QUESTIONS

1. What are the advantages and disadvantages of best friends entertaining being more than just friends?

2. How would you handle choosing between two sets of close friends who don't get along?

3. Do you believe Donovan is too young to express that level of sentiment toward Monica? Explain your answer.

4. Compare and contrast the relationships between Monica and her parents, Donovan and his parents, and Will and his parents. Explain whether or not each pre-teen shares the same type of relationship with both parents. Whose relationship is more beneficial to an adolescent's growth? Explain.

5. Mr. James, Monica's father, seems to be parenting her based on his past mistakes. Is that ethical? Explain your answer. Do you believe your parents sometimes do that? Give an example and whether   it was ethical or not.

6. Explain whether Monica and Donovan were being logical by lying to their parents about the movie outing.

7. Nicole shares with her readers about being in a school where she felt like another negative statistic. Is this a common practice in our educational system? If so, how can students and parents

enforce reform? What do you think your parents would do if you were in a school like Nicole?

8. Explain if it is fair for Mr. James to dictate how he parents based on how he behaved as a child.

9. How would you characterize Donovan's actions at the dance?

10. What scene would you recreate that would change the story line? Explain your reasoning.

11. Do you believe Donovan and Monica will ever recover from this setback? Explain your answer.

12. Which character would you give advice to and why? Be detailed with your response.

13. The setting of this book is the early nineties. Identify any similarities to fashion, music, and places they hung out. Was there anything about this time period you didn't identify with? Complete a WebQuest to learn more about at least two musical artists or   television references that were unfamiliar to you.

ACKNOWLEDGMENTS

God, you allowed me to do this again! Because of you, I have been blessed with a gift. You told me on the way home from an open mic in Charlotte over twenty years ago that I was born to do this! Although this is the first novel, this is the fourth of many books. There is no genre I won't represent because you called me to be a writer.

I'm grateful for my family, including the awesome mother I inherited this gift from, who has always been supportive.

Kyra March, you were pivotal in me finalizing the name for this novel and the rest of the books in the series. You, Ananda, and Yasha's feedback helped me more than you know. I'd like to thank all three of you.

To my current and former students, thank you for being my muses and critics. I also want to specifically acknowledge Ms. Melanie Wood who unknowingly pushed me to finally finish a novel that will be eventually published. When I would share excerpts of novels and writings, the students would always ask, *"When are you going to finish it? When are you going to publish it?"*

My response was normally, *"I'll finish it when I finish it."*

Ms. Melanie is the first student who challenged me by saying, *"You always say you have to finish it but when are you going to finally finish it?"* Your words stayed with me and I'm glad to say this novel is partially due to your indirect nudging.

At Alice Drive Middle School in Sumter, SC, I had friends who would pass around my short stories and novellas. Shalonda Shaw and I had a folder we passed back and forth in seventh grade. Some teachers thought it was notes, and some of them were. Some of the pages of the folder were fictional stories we used to write together. Some of my faithful readers were two of our other friends, Jessica Mellerson and Yvonne Belser. At a class reunion for Sumter High Class of '98, they asked me whatever happened to those stories I wrote! Although surprised they remembered them, they awakened me to a genre of writing I hadn't touched in years and encouraged me to believe in my craft again. I'm forever grateful to you.

Before taking a fiction writing course at Winthrop University, I had written three books. I remember the first one, written in the seventh grade, was in a yellow folder and got confiscated by my best friend's stepmother who handed it over to my mother. I wrote the second one during my eighth grade year, which was the novel Jessica and Yvonne referred to years later at our class reunion. It was in a purple folder that was confiscated by my social studies teacher and handed over to the vice principal at ADMS. He kept it just in case I got in trouble (I didn't get in trouble in school), and I had to speak with our guidance counselor. I wrote another one in high school. All of them contained content that would be deemed inappropriate. Nevertheless, I wanted to be grown and I understood drama.

In college, I completed a fiction writing course that left my ego wounded. I couldn't handle the critiques and just assumed I was never meant to write fiction. I'm eternally grateful for God, family, and friends who reawakened me, reminded and encouraged me that I was created to write fiction.

Mrs. Jeanette Tyson Gregory, you were   my first writing mentor who believed I could publish, even when I didn't believe I could. I still regret not publishing when you gave me the opportunity. Nevertheless, I'm elated God brought you into my life to push me to the next level. Crazy how much I wrote but didn't think about publishing until I met you.

I also want to thank Christian Price who accepted the challenge of being a Beta reader who gave ample feedback.

I would like to salute Tamika Sims who gave me the encouragement I needed to self-publish.

I greatly appreciate my church family, Right Direction Church International who is under the leadership of Bishop Herbert and Dr. Marcia Bailey. Because of your teachings, I keep at my dream despite the obstacles. Being allowed to perform in multiple House of SWATA (talent showcases) and later performing during services and conferences continued to grow my confidence in my gift.

I will never forget when I met you, Mrs. Pamela Harris Gantt. When you performed a poem at the last SWATA open mic at the Family Life Center, I remember God told me I needed to talk to you. You have been my cheerleader since day one and I thank you for your gift and just being an awesome big SWATA (writer) sister! Reading your books kept me pushing.

Mrs. Jerlean Noble, I'm grateful for your wisdom and encouragement. Being a part of the Columbia Writer Alliance has blessed me by helping me mold and cultivate my talent.

If you are an aspiring writer who seeks to be published, I highly encourage that you join this group. You can get more information about them on their website, www.colawriters.info.

ABOUT THE AUTHOR

Rian N. Jenkins has been in love with writing since sixth grade. Over thirty years, she inspired, entertained, and educated many through poetry, novellas, journalism, and performances. In 2021, she added author to her résumé.

She is also a former teacher of twenty years and a spoken word artist, author, mentor and program director of CROWN HER, formerly known as the ROSES mentoring program. To add to the list of dope and magnificent titles that uplift and empower the community, she calls herself a LIT specialist, doing book talks online while sponsoring the All Black Author Book Drive and Giveaway in the Columbia area.

She is a native of Sumter, SC, graduated from Ridge View in '98 in Columbia, SC and Winthrop University in '03. She also has roots in Edisto Island, Hollywood and Saint Helena Island.

She is the mother of a brilliant and talented young king.

To learn more information about her or how to book her for a performance, author visit, writer's workshop or find her on social media, visit her website, www.riannjenkins.com.